# hostage

### Willo Davis Roberts

## Aladdin Paperbacks

**New York London Toronto Sydney Singapore**

First Aladdin Paperbacks edition August 2001
Copyright © 2000 by Willo Davis Roberts
Aladdin Paperbacks
An imprint of Simon & Schuster
Children's Publishing Division
1230 Avenue of the Americas
New York, NY 10020

The Library of Congress has cataloged the hardcover edition as follows:
Roberts, Willo Davis
Hostage/ Willo Davis Roberts.
p.    cm.
"A Jean Karl book."
Summary: When eleven-year-old Kaci interrupts burglars in the
process of robbing her house, she and her nosy elderly neighbor
Mrs. Banducci are kidnapped and held hostage by the desperate and
ruthless criminals.
ISBN 0-689-81669-3 (hc.)
[1. Robbers and outlaws—Fiction. 2. Kidnapping—Fiction.
3. Neighbors—Fiction.] I. Title.
PZ7.R54465HO   2000   [Fic]—dc21   99-20701
ISBN 0-689-84446-8 (Aladdin pbk.)

ISBN 0-689-81669-3 (hc.)
[1. Robbers and outlaws—Fiction. 2. Kidnapping—Fiction.
3. Neighbors—Fiction.] I. Title.
PZ7.R54465HO   2000   [Fic]—dc21   9-20701
ISBN 0-689-84446-8 (Aladdin pbk.)

# Books by Willo Davis Roberts

*The View from the Cherry Tree*

*Don't Hurt Laurie!*

*The Minden Curse*

*More Minden Curses*

*The Girl with the Silver Eyes*

*The Pet-sitting Peril*

*Baby-sitting Is a Dangerous Job*

*No Monsters in the Closet*

*Eddie and the Fairy Godpuppy*

*The Magic Book*

*Sugar Isn't Everything*

*Megan's Island*

*What Could Go Wrong?*

*Nightmare*

*To Grandmother's House We Go*

*Scared Stiff*

*Jo and the Bandit*

*What Are We Going to Do About David?*

*Caught!*

*The Absolutely True Story . . . How I Visited Yellowstone Park with the Terrible Rupes*

*Twisted Summer*

*Secrets at Hidden Valley*

*The Kidnappers*

*Pawns*

*Hostage*

# one

I'm the kind of person who loves being thrilled by a scary book or movie. I like feeling the hairs prickle on the back of my neck and gooseflesh creep along my arms. In the safety of my own living room, or curled up in bed at night, knowing the rest of my family is within shouting distance, I'm as brave as anything. I'll take on lions, and tigers, and bears. I'll tiptoe with the heroine through a darkened, deserted house, with the telephone lines all cut and the poker from the fireplace my only weapon.

This is especially satisfying if I have a big bowl of popcorn beside me, one that I don't have to share with anyone.

Dad says I've got a heck of an imagination. It's about my only personal asset, in a family with brilliant minds and multiple talents. I can't compete with any of them on their own turf. I'm the ugly duckling in a flock of birds of paradise.

Except that I can make up stories, and enjoy the ones other people have made up. Especially the ones calculated to send paralyzing chills through my entire system.

So I always thought I'd be ready for a real adventure, if one ever came along.

I didn't know how stupid an idea that was until it happened.


Dad never really wanted to buy the house in Lofty Cedars Estates. He said all the houses there were too expensive.

Mom said, "I told you, honey. I know we can't swing a new house unless we continue to be a two-income family, but I love being office manager at the clinic. I want to keep on working. I don't mind having to hold down a job in order to meet the payments. Now that the piano is paid for, we'll be able to do more with the money I earn than just have the house. We can put the rest of my salary in the bank, in a college fund for the kids. You know we aren't going to be able to send them to college on our current savings. Not all four of them."

"The houses are ostentatious," Dad countered. "Big, fancy, show-off places. I'm a high school principal, for pete's sake. Not the governor."

"Ken," Mom said patiently, "these are not mansions. They're family homes. They have five bedrooms, three bathrooms. No waiting in line when we're all getting ready for work or school! They have a rec room for the kids as well as a living room for us, where we can listen to our own music and read in peace. Doesn't that sound appealing? Not having to listen to their music?"

Since one of Dad's common complaints was that he didn't like the same kind of music we kids did, he had to admit that would be a plus. "That doesn't take care of ostentatious," he said.

"What's ostentatious?" Wally asked, but nobody paid any attention to him.

"Honey, it doesn't need to be any more ostentatious than we want it to be. They'll let us do our own decorating. We can move our own furniture in. We can use the bedroom sets we already own. We don't have to throw out your old chair, though it would be nice to have it reupholstered if we decide we want to change the colors in the living room."

"There are eight thousand families in this school district. Most of them can't afford a house like the ones in Lofty Cedars. What are they going

3

to say about a principal who thinks he's too good to live like everybody else?"

"There are lots of families already living in Lofty Cedars," I put in. "They're mostly just ordinary working families, like us."

Mom gave me a look that meant, Shut up, Kaci, let me do this my way.

I subsided, and watched my brother Jeff struggling to keep still, too. He really liked Coralee Braden, whose family had just moved into a house three doors down from where they were just building a house Mom wanted.

Dad wouldn't give up. "Lofty Cedars Estates is a stupid name for a housing development." We were all sitting around the dinner table, and he speared another slice of rare roast beef. Mom had chosen her time well, during one of his favorite meals, to bring up the subject of moving. Maybe, though, I thought, she should have waited until we got to the chocolate cake to make sure he was in the best possible mood.

"A stupid name," Mom echoed, momentarily nonplussed. "Why is Lofty Cedars any more stupid than Windy Bluff or Pleasant Acres?"

"Because there aren't any Lofty Cedars, that's why." Dad helped himself to a large scoop of mashed potatoes and ladled brown gravy generously over it while I held my breath.

"Two, Dad," Jodie said. She wanted the new house, too. Her best friend, Marsha, had moved to Phoenix, and she was lonesome. Jodie wanted to make new friends, and she was in the midst of her first crush on a boy, another fifth grader, named Saul Jonas. Saul just happened to live on the first street outside of Lofty Cedars Estates, so she'd have to walk past his house every day coming and going from school. "There's two, remember? Right where you drive into Cedar Lane."

Dad looked up from his plate. "They're ten feet high," he stated. "I wouldn't call that lofty in this part of the country where a lot of cedars get to be eighty or a hundred feet tall."

"You wouldn't want to call them little cedars," Jeff said, forgetting the look I'd just had from Mom. "After all, in just a few years they'll have grown a lot, and before long they'll be lofty."

Mom had had enough. She didn't even bother to squelch Jeff. "The main reason I want to move, Ken," she said in that way she has when she gets serious, "is that I really want to get out of this neighborhood."

"What's wrong with this neighborhood?" Dad wanted to know, getting moderately annoyed at not being able to eat his dinner in peace. "We've lived here for seventeen years, Eve. We've got this house practically paid for!"

"And that's one reason it's feasible to move. We can sell this place and have a good, big down payment on another house. That way the payments won't be all that bad. But the most important thing is what's happening around here. I don't like the way I worry about the kids being out in the evenings, walking to and from friends' houses or a playground. I don't feel safe here anymore. I don't like the way we have to lock our doors every time we go out, and the kids have to carry keys. Mr. Hoskins actually got mugged only a few blocks from here, just a week ago."

"Ed Hoskins is an idiot," Dad said, but his voice had changed a little. "He goes into a bar and shows off a wad of money big enough to choke a billy goat, and then when he's had too much to drink he walks home through a back alley instead of under the streetlights. You really don't feel safe here anymore, Eve?"

"No, honey, I really don't," Mom said, more quietly now.

And that's how we came to buy the house in Lofty Cedars. The house where each of us could have our own room, and be within walking distance of the high school for Jeff, the middle school for me, and the elementary for Wally and Jodie.

Mom admitted, when Dad persisted rather firmly, that we'd still have to lock our doors when we left the house, even in the daytime.

Yet the main thing was that in Lofty Cedars, we'd all be safer. Which goes to show how wrong even the best of parents can be.

Mom was afraid it might take quite a while to sell our old house. But Dad read in the paper that due to the new navy base in Everett, housing was at a premium. Thousands of sailors coming into the area needed homes at a price they could afford, and the article said that the average time it took to sell after putting a house on the market in our county was only fifty-four days. The contractors were building new houses as quickly as they could, but a lot of the navy personnel were already here and desperate to be able to bring their families. A friend from church who was a realtor assured us that selling ours wouldn't be a problem at all. "List it now, and we'll probably have a buyer before school is out for the summer," he told us cheerfully.

We sold it almost too fast, before the house in Lofty Cedars was ready for us. The buyers were a young navy officer and his wife and two little girls, who were moving up from San Diego, and they had friends who had already bought in our neighborhood. Fortunately, they weren't scheduled to move up until fall.

A week after Mom and Dad had accepted their offer, there was a robbery right across the street from our old house.

We had known the Andersons all our lives, and Jeff was good friends with their younger son, Larry. So we knew they were on vacation that week. Mr. Anderson was a history buff and he'd won an all-expense-paid trip to Boston because of a scholarly essay he had submitted to a contest. It was a major prize, so there was a story about it in the *Daily Gazette,* and the whole family was excited about seeing the Constitution and Paul Revere's house and the Old North Church, where lanterns were hung to warn the patriots that the British were coming. There was going to be a follow-up article when they came home that described everything they'd seen.

So we knew their house was empty. Jeff had agreed to go over once a day to feed their two dogs, which he did right after supper every night.

I was the one who saw the lights. Usually I had to be careful about staying up after Jodie had decided to go to sleep, because she liked it dark. But tonight she was sleeping over with Bethany Wightman, a girl she hoped would be a new best friend. Bethany had moved here only recently and hadn't made many friends yet, so her mother had made a point of meeting Mom and sounding her out about the girls getting together. It was a relief to me that she went and I had our room to myself.

I had been reading kind of late, after everyone

else in the family had gone to bed. I got up to get a snack and saw a flicker of light behind the living room drapes across the street.

I stopped and peered more closely out my bedroom window. There it came again, just barely showing where the drapes weren't pulled tightly together.

I put down my sandwich and milk and walked across the hall. I opened the door and called softly, "Jeff? You awake?"

"Huh? Kaci? What's up?"

"Something's going on over at the Andersons'," I said softly, so I wouldn't wake up anyone else.

He sounded groggy. "Something like what?"

"Lights. In the living room."

"I couldn't have left any lights on," Jeff complained, rolling over and sitting up. "I wasn't even in there, just in the kitchen."

"It looked like a flashlight sweeping across the other side of the drapes."

That got him out of bed, and he followed me back to my bedroom. "I don't see anything," he said.

"Wait a minute. There, in the front bedroom upstairs. Did you see it?"

My brother leaned on the windowsill, staring. "Let me put my pants on and get the key. I'll go

over and see if something got left on. I never checked upstairs. They were in a hurry to leave for the airport. They could have overlooked a lamp."

"The first light I saw was downstairs, in the living room. Maybe we'd better wake up Dad."

"Mrs. Anderson probably just forgot to turn one lamp off. No need to get Dad out of bed," Jeff said, and headed for his own bedroom.

"Wait a minute," I said. "What if nobody left a light on? What if there's someone in there who doesn't belong there? I told you, the light I saw first was in the living room, and I only saw the flash of it a couple of times. Like someone was moving around."

"I'll be careful," Jeff said, and was gone.

What should I do now? It seemed the height of stupidity, to me, to go barging into a house that was supposed to be empty but might not be. Dad would have a fit if he knew we were even thinking about such a thing.

I turned out my overhead light so I could stand in darkness to observe, and it was then that I noticed the small truck on the street in front of the Anderson place.

The Andersons had flown to Boston, leaving their cars locked in the garage, so there shouldn't have been any vehicles on the street at all. The truck was light colored, about the size of the ones small businesses use to make deliveries. I couldn't tell if anything was printed on the side to identify it or not. No doubt Jeff would notice it when he got there; he was already going down the stairs.

I hesitated, then waited until he emerged from the front door beneath me. "Jeff!" I called softly, leaning out the window. "There's a truck! Check it out!"

He turned and lifted a hand, then crossed the street, stopping momentarily by the rear of the delivery truck.

Memorizing the license number, I decided. He wouldn't have to write it down. He was used to memorizing long pages of concertos and sonatas for his piano competitions; a simple license number would be a piece of cake.

A moment later he looked up at me again, made a circle with his thumb and forefinger, and disappeared around the other side of the truck.

There were no lights that I could see inside the house now. A slight breeze raised the hairs on my bare arms, or was it apprehension? I wished Jeff had called Dad to go over with him. If burglars were in the Anderson house, who knew how safe he was? Of course he wasn't stupid enough to tackle them; he'd stay out of sight, but still . . .

"Kaci?" Dad's voice from my doorway made me swing away from the window, startled. "What's going on? I thought I heard voices, and then a door closing downstairs. Do you know what time it is? Some of us are trying to sleep."

"I'm sorry, Dad. I saw lights in the Andersons' house, so I woke Jeff up. I wanted him to call you before he went over there, but he said he'd be careful. . . ."

"Was that him I heard leaving the house? Kaci, you both know better than to take chances. Why didn't you wake me up?" In a couple of strides he joined me at the window—a big, bulky shape beside me in the darkness. "Where did you see the lights?"

I told him. He muttered something under his breath. "Let me get some pants on and I'll go over there myself. And if we don't both come back within five minutes, call the police. That's what they're for."

I stayed at my post, wondering if this was important enough to pray about. Grandma Beth, Dad's mother, said everything was important enough for that, that God had plenty of time and the ability to listen to even the smallest concerns, even to praying for catching a bus. Dad said it would make more sense to start for the bus stop five minutes earlier, but Grandma Beth assured him that when she was already doing her best, it couldn't hurt to pray for help when she needed it.

I didn't know if Jeff needed help or not, but if I prayed for his safety and it turned out to be unnecessary, nobody would know except God and me. I had no sooner whispered the words, however, than things started happening down in the street.

The strange truck mostly blocked my view of the Andersons' front door, but I could tell that it opened and three people came out. They were in a hurry. They opened up the back of the truck, put something inside, and one of them climbed in after it. Then another one slammed the door in the back and came around to jump into the driver's seat, and another one scrambled for the opposite door. They took off, leaving the house behind them wide open.

Alarmed, I turned toward the darkened hall, where I heard Dad coming out of his bedroom. He must have pulled his pants on over his pajama bottoms and stuck his feet into shoes without socks, because he'd only been gone a matter of seconds.

"Dad, whoever it was just left!" We heard the squeal of tires as the truck went around the corner. "I don't see Jeff anywhere!"

"Call 9-1-1!" Dad said, and clattered down the stairs without turning on a light.

# two

The police car arrived just as I reached the front door. Mom was calling down from upstairs, wanting to know what was going on, and I turned long enough to reply, "Jeff and Dad are over at the Andersons', and the police are here!" before I ran outside in my bare feet.

An officer unfolded himself from the front seat of the patrol car and turned to look at me. "You the one who called 9-1-1?"

"Yes, sir. The truck that was here just left in a hurry, with three men in it, and my dad and my brother are over there somewhere!"

"Go back into your house, please," the officer said. He didn't wait to see if I obeyed but approached the open door of Andersons' house. I retreated as far as the end of our sidewalk and stood waiting.

The officer called out, and I heard a voice responding. Mom spoke behind me, and I turned to see that she was still wrapping a robe over her nightgown as she emerged from the front door. "Kaci, what's happening? Where's Dad?"

"Over there." It wasn't cold, but I was shivering. I explained to her why there was a patrol car across the street. "The cop told me to stay here."

"He didn't give me any orders," Mom said, and started across the street in her slippered feet. After a moment of hesitation, I decided that I'd probably get away with joining her.

As we neared the Andersons' open doorway, we heard men's voices and detected a light somewhere in the back of the house. Mom hesitated and called out. "Ken?"

"Back here, Eve. Jeff's okay, he just has a knot on his head."

We made our way toward the voices, through the house that I'd been in many times. Tonight nothing looked familiar, and it wasn't just the lack of lights. I rubbed my arms where the hair was standing on end, and looked into the living room as we passed the doorway. For a moment I didn't realize what was wrong, and then I did.

"The TV's gone," I said as I moved into the lighted kitchen area where the uniformed officer and Dad were holding my brother by the arms as he struggled to stand up. "Those guys in the truck must have stolen it! What happened to Jeff?"

"They hit me over the head. From behind," Jeff said painfully. "Knocked me out for a few minutes, I guess."

"I thought you were going to be careful," I said.

"I thought I was being careful," he told me. "Let me sit down a minute, Dad."

They lowered him onto a kitchen chair, where he felt around on the top of his head, wincing. "I sneaked up on the back of the house and peeked into a window, but I couldn't see anything. It was pitch-black in here, so I thought they must be working upstairs, where Kaci and I saw the lights moving around. I decided I'd go back home and call the police, and I had the license number of that truck parked out front. . . ." He drew his fingers away from his head and looked at them, tinged with red. He scowled. "The minute I got to the front corner of the house, somebody lunged out of the shrubbery and hit me with something hard. Real hard."

"You shouldn't have come over here by yourself in the first place," Dad told him. "The police are equipped to handle burglars."

The cop was looking at me. "You said the TV was gone. Are you familiar enough with the house to tell me what else might be missing?"

I hesitated. "Maybe. Jeff spends more time over here than I do."

"Would you mind walking through the house with me to see what else is missing? Both of you?"

So we did. Mom and Dad came along, and we all noticed empty spaces where items had been taken. Three TVs, a computer and a printer, a microwave, silverware.

"It makes me feel as if I'm the intruder," Mom said ruefully when she pulled out the drawer where the real silver was kept. "But I've been here at parties and seen where they keep this stuff. And, sure enough, it's gone. Oh, my, Ruby's going to be so upset. That was her grand-mother's silver. Do you think there's any chance of getting it back?"

"We'll try," the cop said, but from the look on his face I didn't think he had much hope of it.

By the time we came back downstairs, Jeff was ready to sit down again. "Oh, boy. How am I going to tell them what a lousy job I did of taking care of their house? The fool dogs didn't even bark, and if it hadn't been for Kaci noticing there was someone over here, we wouldn't have a clue anything had been taken. How did the thieves know the place was empty and they could just walk in and help themselves?"

Dad's tone was wry. "The fact that they were taking this big trip to Boston was in the newspaper, remember? Advertising, pure and simple."

The cop nodded, putting away the notebook in which he'd been taking notes. "Had one couple of weeks ago. Somebody cleaned out the household of a prominent family while they were at a well-publicized funeral for the lady's father. Isolated house, and they knew there wouldn't be anybody there for at least a couple of hours, so they backed up their truck."

Mom was appalled. "Did you recover any of their belongings?"

"No, ma'am. Not so far. You may be asked to come down to the station and answer a few more questions tomorrow, verify that license number. If you can locate the name of the hotel where the Andersons are staying, it would be helpful."

"I have it written down, I think," Jeff said. He couldn't seem to keep from touching the lump on his head.

"I think we'd better go clean up that cut," Mom said. "Make sure it doesn't need sutures." Anybody else would have said "stitches," but she works in a medical office.

"First I want to check on the dogs. See if

they're okay. I don't understand why they didn't bark."

I went with him to the kennel in the back of the lot, and that's when we found out the dogs had been drugged.

I was more indignant about that than about the burglary. The Andersons might get their stuff back, and they carried insurance against thefts, but they'd be devastated if their dogs died.

"They're still breathing," Jeff stated, kneeling beside Mickey, the big collie. "I hope it was just something to put them to sleep, not to kill them. The thieves probably threw them some drugged meat. I wonder if we can get a vet to look at them this time of night?"

Dad did. He even carried Mickey out to our van while Jeff brought Henry, the little beagle, who was so limp, I began to pray that he wouldn't die. Mom inspected the bump on Jeff's head before she decided it wasn't all that serious and he could go along to the vet's. When I wanted to go, too, she frowned, but finally agreed that I could. She knew I was scared for the dogs.

The vet said the dogs had probably been poisoned rather than just drugged to keep them quiet. He told us he'd have to keep them overnight and he might not know until morning whether they'd pull through or not, so we went home feeling pretty glum about the whole thing. I didn't envy Jeff having to report to the Andersons that not only had their house been robbed but that their dogs were dead.

That was definitely something worth praying about. I did, all the way home.

Jeff called the vet first thing in the morning and was told that both dogs were doing better and that the vet thought they'd be all right. I didn't know if my prayers had helped, but I thought they must have; both Mickey and Henry had looked as if they were already dead when we'd delivered them to the veterinary hospital.

Sometimes I'd wished that we were home schooled, like the Anderson kids, so that we could take vacations any time of year. Now I was glad they were still in Boston, so we didn't have to face them immediately. At least by the time they got home their pets would be perfectly all right again.

We weren't going to get any vacation this summer, it seemed, when our school was finally over. Some people think that school principals have long vacations from their work, with nothing to do. That sure wasn't true of Dad. He had so many things to attend to at school, even when it wasn't in session, that we didn't see him much more than during the school year. There were committees to meet with, new teachers to be interviewed and hired, supervising of maintenance of the grounds and buildings, and working with the group trying to persuade the public that we needed to pass a bond issue for a new science lab.

And this year we had to get ready to move, too. The people who bought our house didn't need it until fall. Even so, when my parents signed the papers to buy the new house, Mom had hoped we'd be able to move in long before school started again. But things kept happening to put off the moving date.

Even when the house seemed finished, there were problems. First the contractor couldn't seem to get all the interior painting finished. Everybody agreed that it would be much more difficult to do with our furniture moved in, so we had to wait on that. Then the carpet Mom wanted in the living room was out of stock in the color she'd asked for. So we had to wait for that. Then the man who was supposed to install the appliances was in a car accident and broke several bones. They couldn't find anyone else in his company to replace him, so we waited most of the rest of the summer for his bones to heal.

Dad didn't care much one way or the other when we moved, as long as nobody bothered him to do anything about it. Mom said it would be much easier if we got in and settled before school opened, and she was frustrated when people kept promising things would be ready at a certain time and then they weren't.

We were all ready to move. I was eager to go because I hated sharing a room with Jodie. I'd have a room to myself in the new house, and Mom had let me select my own colors.

Jodie is the beauty of the family. She is fussy about everything around her being beautiful, too. Three of my aunts had gone together to get her the bedspreads and curtains and everything that went with them for her ninth birthday. Unfortunately, I got to "enjoy" them, too. Ruffled pink and white checks, with embroidered rosebuds. I felt as out of place in that room as a kumquat in a bouquet of roses.

Jodie, of course, looked perfect in that delicate setting. And she kept the room perfectly in order. Everything I did was wrong, from leaving my orange sweater lying where it clashed with the pink and white checks to piling books on the elegant white dresser or nightstand. And instead of a decent reading lamp, I had this cute little deal that wouldn't take more than a sixty-watt bulb, with a ruffled pink-and-white-checked shade.

So I was ecstatic about the prospect of privacy,

bookcases that held books instead of Barbies and stuffed toys, and a cool blue-and-white room without ruffles.

We each had to pack our own things to move, and some of my stuff had been in boxes most of the summer. But there was still plenty to do when we finally got the word that we could start moving in the following weekend, the one just after school started.

My friend Nancy came over to help me. But before we started pulling things out of the closet, she had something to tell me. "Didn't you say the truck that hauled away the Andersons' stuff was plain white, kind of small?"

"Yes, why?" I looked up from the sweater in my hands, trying to decide whether it was worth keeping or if I should put it in the bag for the Salvation Army.

"Well, on the way over here I saw a truck that sort of looked like you'd described. Only it had a logo painted on the side and the back. A symbol of a couple of tall trees, pines or something. And it said, 'Evergreen Industries,' and had a phone number. I wondered if it could be the same truck. I mean, they could have painted on the other stuff after they left here if they wanted to keep on using it."

"Jeff gave the license number to the police," I

reminded her. "Seems like in the last couple of months they'd have spotted it if it were still around."

"Ever hear of changing plates?" Nancy asked. "It's only over on Statler Street. You want to go take a look at it?"

It didn't seem likely that the same truck would be in use in broad daylight for the same purpose, I thought, but what the heck. It wouldn't hurt to check it out. I decided the sweater was too tight for me, and it wasn't pink so Jodie wouldn't like it, so I dropped it in the giveaway bag. "Let's go," I said.

Approaching the parked truck from the front, it did look pretty much like the one that had driven off with the Andersons' stuff. It gave me a creepy feeling. But when we got close enough to read the license number, it wasn't the one Jeff had memorized. "I'm sure it didn't have anything painted on the sides, either," I told Nancy. "Otherwise, it could be it."

Across the street a birthday party was in progress. There were a couple of dozen little kids with balloons, and they were being entertained by a clown doing acrobatics. They were eating ice cream and cake off paper plates, and as we watched, one little girl allowed her plate to tilt. The ice cream slid off and landed in the lap of a small boy sitting near her feet, and he let out a howl.

One of the mothers came with a washcloth and some more ice cream, and somebody else stepped in what had been spilled on the grass, and for a few minutes we were distracted, seeing how it would all come out.

And then we walked alongside the white truck, and Nancy said, "It looks like it was just freshly painted, don't you think?"

"Yeah," I said slowly. "And hastily, too. See where they didn't quite get that corner?" I glanced toward the house in front of which it was parked, but nobody seemed to be watching us. "I think I'll write down this license number and give it to Dad. Maybe the police can look it up. In case it's been changed, they could check on this one."

We turned around and returned to my house, followed by shrieks of laughter from the birthday party. When we looked back from the corner, there was the clown doing cartwheels for the little kids.

"You ever have a party with a clown to entertain?" I asked, and Nancy shook her head.

"I only ever had two parties in my whole life," she told me. "I had to beg for those, and Mom said it was too much work to do anything fancy."

Nobody else was around when we got home except for Jeff, who was practicing. He practices at least four hours a day, which means he almost never has to do any chores like the rest of us. He's as good as anyone I ever saw on TV. He was in the middle of the really fast and difficult piece he was going to play in the competition in October, so I knew he wouldn't want to be interrupted. We went on past the living room and upstairs.

Nancy was looking dreamy. "He plays like an angel, doesn't he?"

"Yeah, he's pretty good. But grumpy if we distract him."

"I guess geniuses are entitled to have their eccentricities," Nancy excused him.

"Geniuses are a pain to live with sometimes," I retorted. "Here, I've nearly filled this box. Let's put all my shorts and jeans in that one, and I'll carry everything on hangers just the way they are, in the back of the van."

When Dad came home, I gave him the slip with the license number on it. "I just thought it might be worth checking on," I told him. "In case it's the same truck."

He looked at it and nodded. "Good thinking. I'll pass it along to the police. Might not do much good, it's been so long, but it can't hurt. I've got some paperwork, so I'll be in the den. Would you be a good sport and get me something cold to drink, Kaci? Oh, hi, Nancy, how's everything at your house?"

"Dull," Nancy said. "Same as always. Nobody in our family ever has an adventure."

"Count your blessings," he said, as we'd heard her say this so many times, and she had to laugh.

While we got Dad a tall iced tea, we each got ourself a can of pop, and I picked up a box of those fancy crackers we keep on hand for Grandma Beth when she comes over. "To tide us over until supper," I said, handing the crackers to Nancy.

Dad was hanging up the phone when we delivered his tea. "Looks like your suspicions might have been worth something," he said. "That license number belongs to a truck that was stolen two days ago on the other side of town, and it wasn't a white truck. I told them where you saw it, and they're checking it out."

But by the time the police got there, the truck was gone. The birthday party was over, and nobody nearby had noticed who had driven the truck away.

Dad sighed after talking to the police a second time, just as we were having dinner. "Maybe Mom is right. Maybe it *is* time to get out of this neighborhood. I hate to see anyplace in this town not safe for families to live in, but I guess it's reality today. Crime is up everywhere."

Mom didn't say, "I told you so." She felt bad about it, too. We had lots of friends in the few blocks around our old house, and of course we knew someone else was moving into it with a family. "It almost makes me feel guilty," she confessed as she was testing the spaghetti. "If it isn't safe for us, it isn't any safer for anyone else."

"Do you think the people with the stolen truck are the same ones who robbed the Andersons, since it was the same kind of truck?" I asked at dinner.

Nobody knew, of course. The Andersons had been horrified about the loss of their TVs and computer equipment, and even more upset about the poisoning of their dogs. They didn't blame Jeff, though, and they paid him the agreed-upon sum, which made him feel guilty. Not enough so that he didn't take the money, though. They hoped to get at least the antique silverware back. But so far nothing had turned up.

Jodie had just come home from dancing lessons and was still in her pretty pink outfit. Her blond curls jiggled when she moved her head. Even I had to admit she was charming to look at. I happened to know she had a tendency to pinch when nobody was looking, and to snitch whatever I'd hidden for my snacks, and to close my library books so I had to look for my place. "At least the insurance paid for all the things that were stolen, didn't it, Daddy?"

"Yes. But it's not like anybody's getting off free, you know. The reason insurance costs so much is that the insurance company has to pay out claims for losses. In the end, it means we all have to pay more for everything we insure. Wally, watch what you're doing, son. You just dragged your sleeve through your gravy."

Wally swiped at himself with a napkin. "Did I tell you our team is playing the Wildcats Friday night, Dad? Can you come watch?"

"I hope so, son. I'll try to see most of the game before my meeting, all right? But remember we're moving this weekend."

Jodie didn't like the attention to be drawn away from her. "On Saturday I'm in the dance recital. Everybody's coming to that, aren't they?"

"Of course," Mom said, "moving or not, we're coming." She looked at Dad. He didn't announce another conflict, but asked her, "Whose idea was it for us to have four kids?"

She laughed. "Yours, I think. Listen up, kids. Every spare moment you have, pack up all your belongings so we'll be all ready to go. That means you, too, Jodie. I'm glad that Bethany is your best friend, but moving comes first, so plan to do your share. Okay?"

# three

We hadn't made it before school started, so that first week I still got to walk to school with Nancy. It was kind of bittersweet, knowing we were doing it for the last times. We were both in middle school. In elementary we had been the oldest class, but now in sixth grade we were the babies, practically.

"The eighth graders are so arrogant!" I told Nancy. "As if they run the whole school!"

"Oh, well," she said. "Wait until next year. When they move up to senior high, *they*'ll be the infants."

So much of my stuff was packed that it was hard to find anything to put on, and of course everybody else was wearing their best at the beginning of school. Most of them had something new during the first week, but Mom said we didn't have time to shop until after we got settled into the new house, so I felt self-conscious in my old stuff that everybody had seen a million times.

It was a relief when Mom announced at dinner, "The bedrooms are finished. Tomorrow afternoon I'll take over a load of everything that's packed."

"How many days' worth of underwear do I have to keep here?" I asked. "Are we going to actually be moved in by Saturday? In spite of Jodie's recital?" I was wondering if I could smuggle a paperback book in and read instead of watching all the twirling of pastel flowers and fairies on the stage. Jodie was going to be a tulip. Pink, of course.

"I think so. The recital's only about an hour. Jeff, I notice you still have a pile of music to pack up, so you'd better get at that. The piano mover is scheduled to be here Friday afternoon."

"If the piano goes, so do I," Jeff said. "Is there any reason why I can't stay over there Friday night?"

Nobody told me how much underwear to save out. Instead, they were talking about all the interesting things everyone else had lined up to do, and how to work out the schedule. I picked at the rest of my dinner and wondered how come nothing thrilling ever happened to me. No Little League games, no dance recitals—though I'd have been petrified if I'd had to get up on the stage and perform, either dancing or playing the piano—no one of the opposite sex watching me with admiration. It seemed as if nobody wanted my input on anything. The only thing I had that was different was my once-a-week allergy shot, and I would just as soon not need that.

I wished something exciting would happen to me.

I should have remembered what Grandma Beth said. "Be careful what you pray for," she told me once. "You might get it."

I wasn't praying for anything special, of course. Just wishing, rather wistfully.

Mom and we kids made most of the arrangements for moving. Dad wasn't about to be stuck with packing and actually hauling things across town to Lofty Cedars Estates. Those things were up to the rest of us.

Our house is always crazy in the mornings when everyone's getting ready to leave for the day. On Thursday morning Wally couldn't find his shoes. Jodie was banging on the bathroom door demanding that Jeff hurry up. Mom got an emergency call from a patient at the clinic where she worked. I heard her explaining, for the millionth time since she'd worked there, that she didn't have Mr. Wortman's chart, and he'd have to call her back after she got to work, and she'd tell Dr. Layton as soon as he came in.

She rolled her eyes as she stuck four more slices of bread in the double-sized toaster, and poured herself a cup of coffee. "I don't know why they think I can help them from here, when all the pertinent information is in their charts at the office. It's one of the things I love about a small town. Anybody can get your home phone number. Kaci, you're not going to wear that to school, are you?"

I glanced down at my old jeans and T-shirt. "Yeah, I intended to. We're going to be painting posters today. I don't want to wreck anything good."

Mom sighed. "All right. Wally, did you look behind that pile of book bags? Maybe your shoes are under there."

"I did," Wally said. "I only found one of them."

"Then keep looking. You're running out of time." She raised her voice. "Jodie, stop pounding on that door! And, Jeff, get out of there as soon as you can!"

Dad came in in time to harvest the toast and start buttering it, then opened the refrigerator. "Isn't there any orange juice?"

"Jeff drank the last of it. You'll have to mix up some more. I took a can out of the freezer."

"I don't have time. I'll settle for coffee. Kaci, you're not wearing those ratty-looking jeans to school, are you?"

I explained again about the poster painting, helping myself to jam for a slice of the toast. He sighed, too. When he raised his voice, everybody else shut up. "Jodie, be quiet! Jeff, hurry up!"

Jeff came out at last, letting Jodie into the bathroom. He was halfway through the kitchen when he stopped and looked at me. "Kaci, you're not going to school like that, are you?"

I blew my bangs off my forehead. "I'm going to be painting posters today," I said through my teeth. I glared at Wally, who had finally found his second shoe behind Dad's briefcase beside the front door. "Aren't you going to bawl me out, too, for wearing these pants?"

"I don't care what you wear," Wally said with a sunny smile. "Isn't there any more juice?"

"I'll mix it," I volunteered, because it was the only way I'd get any. Mom was already draining her cup, looking at her watch and moving.

"If anybody gets a chance to pick up another gallon of milk, Shoefelds' has it on sale today. See you tonight."

"Mom," Jodie said quickly before she could

leave, "I'm going over to Bethany's after school, okay?"

Mom frowned. "No. Mrs. Wightman is working. She won't be home after school. You know the rules, Jodie. No adult at home at her house and you can't go over there. Call me when you get home, the same as always."

"But, Mom, we want to work on our costumes for the school play! We won't do anything we aren't supposed to!"

"Jodie, you know the rules," Mom said. "Call me the minute you get home."

That didn't keep my sister from sounding stressed as she persisted. "Mom, did you know they're going to be making a movie out by Boardman Lake for the next couple of weeks? All the stars are going to be there. Even Evan Soldic! You know, from that new TV show? And the public can come to watch, and maybe even be one of the extras. Could somebody take me out there one afternoon? Please, Mom? Me and Bethany. Please!"

"No, Jodie, I can't take time off work for anything like that," Mom told her. "Just call as usual after school, all right? I have to run. Bye."

"Me, too," Dad said, pushing back his chair. "Get a move on, kids. It doesn't look good for the children of a school principal to be late. I'll call when I know when I can get home for supper, okay? Oh, hi, Nancy, go on in. Kaci will be ready in a minute."

Nancy passed my parents as she came into the kitchen and slumped in the chair Dad had just vacated. "Is anybody going to eat that last slice of toast?"

"Help yourself." I turned off the blender and poured the juice into a tall glass. "Want some of this?"

"Sure. All we had at our house this morning was grapefruit, and Mom won't buy the kind that's sweetened."

We finished eating and set off for school—the next-to-last time we'd walk together.

We hauled two vans' worth of boxes over right after supper on Thursday night. Then, on Friday night, while Wally was helping the Frogs by walloping his first grand-slam home run, I packed up just about everything else I had left. I couldn't drive it over to the new house, of course, but Nancy came by, and we decided to walk over and put away what we could that had already been delivered.

The piano movers had come and taken Jeff's precious instrument. He was already over there with them, telling them where to put it, so we didn't need a key to get in.

It was a nice evening, and people were out working on their lawns or their flowers, and kids were playing in the streets and various yards. There wasn't much traffic, though, and maybe that's why we noticed the old black sedan cruising slowly along our new street in Lofty Cedars.

It was out of place. There were cars parked in most of the driveways or on the street in front of the new houses. Almost all of them were late, expensive models, or if they were older ones, they'd been well taken care of. We saw one man polishing up a 1948 Ford, almost an antique by my standards, and it was a beautiful car.

But the black sedan was beat up and scarred, with the left rear fender crumpled as if it had been backed into something. That made it stand out.

There were three people in it. High school-age boys, I thought, though I didn't get a very good look at their faces. I wondered if they—or one of them—might be moving here to the new subdivision, too.

Not that it would do me any good. Boys Jeff's age or older weren't going to look twice at a skinny sixth grader. I didn't have the least bit of shape yet.

When we got close to our house, we noticed an old lady watering her front lawn with a hose in her hand. She looked at us sharply as we came even with her.

"You girls part of the family moving in at number eighty-seven?" she asked.

"I am," I told her politely. The piano movers' van was just backing out of our new driveway, and the old black sedan slowed to allow it plenty of turning room. "I'm Kaci Drummond."

The lady was wearing an old-fashioned cotton print housedress, the kind of thing my great-grandmother used to wear in our family snapshots. Grandma Beth wore jeans and sweatshirts except when she went to church or to weddings.

"I'm Carrie Banducci," she told us. Her white hair was drawn back in a bun. Her eyes were bright blue, looking younger than the rest of her. "You have a big family, do you?"

"Mom and Dad and four kids," I said, hoping she didn't object to that.

"Someone plays the piano, I see," she observed.

"My brother Jeff," I agreed.

"And what does your father do?"

"He's principal of the high school."

"And that was your mother I saw carrying in boxes earlier? In the blue van?"

I nodded, ready to go on, but she took a step

along with us. "And does she work, too? So many women do, these days. In my day we stayed home and took care of our kids."

"She manages the medical clinic on Third Street," I conceded, feeling compelled to pause politely. I refrained from telling her that Mom took pretty good care of us even if she did have a job.

Mrs. Banducci sprayed water out over the sidewalk to wash away some recently cut grass. Either her aim wasn't very good, or she intended to get our feet wet. I was glad I was wearing my old athletic shoes. Nancy had on a good pair of sandals and danced backward to get out of the way of the water.

Mrs. Banducci didn't seem to notice. "I saw the delivery truck a little earlier. You're getting a new TV, I guess."

I was beginning to be irritated. "Yes. We're going to need a second one, for the family room."

"The people across the street, the Lowerys, bought a new TV, too. A fifty inch." I wondered if she'd gone over and inspected it to be sure of the size.

"I only need one," Mrs. Banducci stated, twisting the hose the other way so that it was now splashing our newly seeded lawn. "For my soaps, you know."

"It's a big house for one person," Nancy said, looking up at it. "Or do you have a husband?"

I wanted to smack her. Why was she keeping this conversation going? Who cared if the old woman lived alone or had a husband in her big house?

"Jamison died twelve years ago," Mrs. Banducci said. "He was seventy-two, and he had a heart attack and died. He was six years older than I was, so maybe I'll die soon, too. Maybe not, though. Women have a longer life span. Seventy-eight isn't terribly old these days."

"Excuse us, we need to go," I told her, but right then she looked past me with a faint scowl. "Who are those boys? In that dreadful old car? I've seen them here several times in the past few days, just driving in and out of the subdivision. I'm sure they don't live here, so what reason do they have for being here? Didn't they just drive past a minute or two ago?"

"Uh-huh. Looking for girls, probably," Nancy offered. "Teenage boys don't need any more reason than that for doing anything. There are quite a few teenage girls here."

"Hmm. They don't look old enough to drive. The deliveryman who brought the appliances for the Sandifords' house—that's the pale yellow one two houses up—hardly looked old enough to have a license. I don't know what the authorities are thinking of, letting people drive when they're so young."

Privately I thought that anyone under fifty probably looked young to her. "Come on, Nancy, let's go see where Jeff decided to put the piano."

"It's nice to see polite young girls moving in next door," Mrs. Banducci told us. "Boys tend to be so wild these days. The DeMonicos—the pale pink house over there with the brick trim—they have five boys." She shook her head. "And two of them have motorcycles. I wouldn't be surprised if they drive everyone crazy with the sound of those motorcycles."

By this time we were walking away from her, but she continued talking to our backs. "Of course, you should see the mother. In my day a woman who dyed her hair red was suspect just on that score. And she wears bright purple! Can you imagine, purple with that red hair!"

I spoke out of the corner of my mouth to Nancy as we walked up the driveway to our new place, "How did we luck out and get her for a neighbor? Listen, Jeff's practicing already."

Much as I admired my brother's talent and his dedication to becoming a professional pianist, I was glad I wasn't the one who had to spend hours every day pounding away at the keyboard.

Nancy, however, had nothing but admiration. We let ourselves into the house, still smelling of paint and new carpeting, and I knew if I let her, she'd sit down on the beautiful blue floor and just listen to him for the rest of the evening.

There was nothing else to sit on, actually. The big living room, twice the size of our old one, was empty except for the grand piano. The instrument glistened with black lacquer that didn't have a scratch on it, and if anyone even approached it as if they might set something on it, or lean against it, or leave a fingerprint on the mirror-like finish, they heard from Jeff in a hurry. Or from Mom, if she was there.

The piano was the most expensive object in our house. Even with the bonuses Mom had saved up for five years at the clinic, and the generous donation from Grandma Beth, it had required some sacrifice on the part of the entire family to pay for it. Mom said it was an investment in Jeff's future. Now that it was completely paid off, the extra money could be concentrated on other things for the new house.

I wished there was something promising in my future that would be considered worth some kind of sacrifice.

Jeff came to a thunderous conclusion and

spun around on the bench to face us. "Hi. For once something got delivered right when it was supposed to. The TV is here, too, but it's still in the box. I didn't know where Mom wanted them to put it. If they have it in here, they won't be able to watch it when I'm practicing. Or I won't be able to play if they're watching. Was the old lady next door still out there watering her lawn?"

"I thought there were automatic sprinklers in all these new lawns," I said, leaning against the wall.

"There are. But I think she likes sprinkling by hand so she can keep track of what's going on in the neighborhood. I guess she's lonely."

"Why did she move into a big house all by herself, then?" I wondered aloud. "She's old enough to go into one of those places for retired people where there are lots of other senior citizens to talk to."

"She told me all about it," Jeff said, flexing his fingers. "Her son bought the house as an investment. He wants her to live in it until he can sell it. He figures the value will go up and in a year or so he'll make a handsome profit. And she doesn't want to live in a place where there are only old people."

"She's close to eighty herself," Nancy said incredulously. "How old does she figure she has to get before she associates with other old people?"

"So she got to you, too," I said. "She seems to know details about everybody who's already moved into Lofty Cedars."

"She'll be talking about us, too," Jeff predicted, "so watch what you do and say."

"I've never done or said anything out of line in my entire life," I told him. "Come on, Nancy, let's get my boxes unloaded, as much as we can before the dressers get delivered."

I heard him hooting with laughter as we went up the stairs.

"It's true," I told my friend as we opened the first box and decided there was nowhere to put any of the things in it except for a few items in the bathroom. "Other people get involved in things that win them awards and commendations, or written up in the paper, stuff that other people find interesting to read about or talk about. I'm so blah, nobody cares what I do or think."

Nancy contemplated a small vase. "You want this in your bedroom? I'll set it on the windowsill for now. Jeff's probably right, Kaci. That old lady next door will keep her eye open for something she can talk to the neighbors about."

I grunted. "She'll have a long wait before there's anything to say about me," I insisted.

Downstairs, Jeff had worked the kinks out of the muscles of his arms and hands and was pounding away again, the music swelling as if he were a full symphony instead of a fifteen-year-old student. I was proud of my brother, but I still wished I had a talent of my own.

When I left the new house Monday morning, we were moved in and a moving van was just pulling up to one of the houses down the block. Someone else had bought a new house and was arriving.

Curious, I stared openly as I approached. They had little kids—there was a tricycle being handed down—which might mean there were baby-sitting possibilities. There isn't much else a girl not yet twelve can do to earn money. It might pay to go introduce myself this afternoon, before every other girl in the development got there first.

Now the men on the truck were unloading furniture. New furniture, by the look of it. I wondered if the people in Lofty Cedars would be willing and able to pay higher rates for baby-sitters than those in our old neighborhood.

A dark green van drove up in front of the moving van, and a lady in jeans got out. She was blond and pretty, younger than Mom, and she gave me a friendly smile.

"Hi," I said, hoping she'd remember me when I came over later. I heard the spatter of water on the sidewalk behind me and turned to see Mrs. Banducci watering her lawn again, eyes fixed on the newcomers. Was it possible to drown a lawn completely? If more people kept moving in around us, Mrs. Banducci's grass might be a casualty.

Nancy and I couldn't walk to school together since I'd moved, but we met a block from school. "My grandma's coming to live with us," she greeted me glumly.

"What's so bad about that? I wouldn't mind if Grandma Beth came to our house," I said. "She's really neat, and she takes my side in arguments and cooks terrific lasagna and cookies."

"My grandma criticizes everything we do. Not just me, all of us. Mom can take it all right, but Dad gets pretty irritated with her. It's a good thing he won't be the one who's home with her all day, or he'd explode. He doesn't think Mom will last for long, either, but Mom says nobody can afford one of those retirement complexes. Grandma isn't sick, but she just can't take care of herself very well anymore."

"At least you have a bedroom for her. You won't have to share."

Nancy shuddered. "Can I come live with you

if it comes to that? You're lucky to have such a great family, Kaci. Everybody in your family is normal."

"Whatever normal is. Did you read all of chapter three today for that test?"

She made a face. "I hate tests."

"So do I."

"But you always get good grades. Unless my paper has an A, I won't dare display it at home. Grandma thinks everybody should be perfect."

We were in a mob of kids by the time we got to the school grounds. It was a beautiful fall day, cool and sunny, and we trooped into the building with everybody else, regretting the end of summer and long, empty days to fill any way we liked.

We were halfway down the long corridor to Room 106 when Mrs. Janacek came out of our homeroom. She smiled and greeted us. "Ready for the first test of the year?" she asked. "I'll bet you both worked all weekend studying for it."

"I'll bet we didn't," Nancy said, and our teacher laughed. We were both glad we'd gotten Mrs. Janacek for our teacher this year. The other half of the sixth grade got Miss Mills, who was a lot older, about a hundred pounds heavier, and who had five o'clock shadow every afternoon even if she did shave her chin. We had all our classes except for music, art, and physical education in our homerooms, so it was important to get a teacher we really liked.

Three boys came tearing down the hall, yelling and running into people, and Mrs. Janacek put out a hand to stop the first one, grabbing him by the arm and swinging him around so that the second boy ran into him.

"Boys, you know better than this! We don't allow running in the halls."

One of them said something rude, and her grip on his arm tightened. I could tell by his face that it was uncomfortable. "That's enough, Stuart. All of you, it's time you were in your classrooms."

Behind her, Miss Mills stepped into the hallway. "What's going on?" she demanded.

"It's under control," Miss Janacek said firmly, and turned the boy around, heading him toward his own room. The others sort of melted away.

I dumped my backpack on the floor under my chair and got a pencil out of the outside pocket of it as the test papers were passed out. I got through the test all right, but before I handed in my paper my nose was running and my eyes were watery and itchy. Mrs. Janacek looked up at me and said, "You need a Kleenex, Kaci?"

I helped myself to a handful from the box on

her desk. "Allergies, I guess. I think it's all those leaves the maintenance men are burning, and having the windows open so the smoke comes in."

We closed the windows in our room, but I got worse and Nancy looked at me in alarm. "I thought you were having allergy shots."

"I didn't have one yet this week. I'm due on Tuesday," I said. "I wonder if it would help to wash my eyes out with a wet paper towel?"

Usually my allergy shots took care of such problems, so I didn't carry the nasal spray with me, but today my eyes continued to stream and itch until I thought I'd go crazy. Finally I decided I'd have to do something.

"Um . . . Mrs. Janacek? I have some medicine at home that can really help this. Do you think I could go home to get it? I could be back before lunchtime is over."

She looked at my reddened face and eyes. "You do look pretty miserable. Why don't you check in with Mrs. Burton to see what she thinks?"

Mrs. Burton is the school nurse. She seemed like a no-nonsense sort of person. She had me sit down, gave me some more tissues, and brought me a wet washcloth to bathe my face. It felt better while I was doing it, but I could see myself in the mirror across the room: I was still a mess.

"Couldn't I go home and use my spray?" I asked.

She considered. Kids aren't usually allowed to go home once they get to school unless they're practically dead. Maybe I looked as if I were. "Why don't I check with your mother to see what she thinks?" the nurse suggested.

She let me talk to Mom on the phone. "I'd come to get you, but we're having a major emergency right now," she said distractedly. "Yes, let me talk to Mrs. Burton. I think you could just run home to get your medication. You know where it is, don't you?"

"In the drawer in my nightstand," I said, and sneezed four times in a row while the nurse was talking to my mother.

So that was how I came to be at our new house in the middle of the day when nobody expected me to be there.

# four

We don't have enough lockers to go around at our middle school, even if we double up on them, so only the eighth graders have them. The rest of us have to carry our junk around with us all day in backpacks. Dad's concerned about it because he says we're all going to need a chiropractor because we try to carry too much.

I didn't usually carry anything but my books, notebook, and my lunch. I almost didn't mind the weight of my backpack because it looked so good. It was waterproof and had outside pockets for pencils and pens and my student body card and tissues and change in case I needed to use a phone or something. And it was bright red.

My grandma got one for each of us before school started. If Mom had picked them out, each would have been different from all the others so we couldn't get them mixed up. As it was, Jodie's and mine were the same. And so far, it hadn't been a problem. But as I went home, I wished I could have left it in school somewhere. It was heavy. I was glad I had it, though, when I had to dig out some tissues, because I had a couple more sneezing spells.

Nearing home, I saw that Mrs. Banducci was putting something into her mailbox out on the curb.

I hoped she'd go inside before I got there, but of course she didn't. She just waited for me to get to her.

"What are you doing home this time of day?" she wanted to know.

I blew my nose again and stuck the soggy Kleenex in one of the outside pockets of the backpack. "I came home to get my allergy medicine." I sneezed and groped for another tissue. "I have to hurry up and get back to school, though."

"I noticed you had another furniture delivery," Mrs. Banducci said. "I couldn't tell what it was. It was in several big boxes."

She was waiting for me to tell her what the delivery had been.

"I don't know," I said truthfully. "I didn't think we were getting anything else."

"They were really big boxes," she said. "A big yellow truck. I couldn't make out what it said on the side."

"I don't know," I repeated. "Excuse me. I have to hurry."

"Was there anyone home to accept delivery?" she asked, taking a few steps along with me when I started moving.

"I don't know. If Mom was expecting something, maybe she came home for a few minutes."

"Her car wasn't there," Mrs. Banducci said. Her eyes were very bright with curiosity.

"I don't know," I said again, feeling another sneeze coming. "Excuse me."

This time I got away from her, though she hadn't gone into her house yet. I glanced back when I went up to the front door and fished around for my key.

To my surprise, I didn't need it. When I touched the knob, it turned, letting me into the front hallway. Maybe Mom was still here. "Mom?" I yelled. Maybe someone had dropped her off and was going to pick her up in a few minutes.

There was no answer. I glanced into the living room as I reached the doorway, and sure enough, there were several huge boxes sitting in the middle of the floor.

I was curious, too, and I went over and opened the nearest carton.

It was empty. Hmm. If they'd already un-loaded, why had they left the boxes like this?

The other two were also empty, and I didn't see anything new that could have come out of them.

I sneezed and shrugged and went on upstairs to get my nasal spray. By the time I'd walked around to the opposite side of the bed, my eyes were so red and watery, I got a washcloth and wrung it out with cold water to press against my face.

Since I'd started the allergy shots I didn't have problems like this very often, and usually the worst of it was in the spring, when everything was blooming and there was lots of pollen around. When I needed the spray, I was supposed to put one squirt in each nostril, and it usually worked pretty fast.

I sat down on the edge of the bed and kept bathing my face while I waited for the spray to take effect. I was sort of gloating over my new blue and white bedroom, with no ruffles and no stuffed toys except my old childhood teddy bear, Oscar, that I'd had since I was two years old. I didn't play with him anymore, of course, but I kept him sitting on top of my dresser with an open book on his lap. Every so often I changed the book so he wouldn't get bored. Today the book was a fascinating one titled *Small Steps: The Year I Got Polio,* by Peg Kehret, a true story about the author's ordeal with a terrible disease when she was only a little bit older than I was.

Oscar was bent slightly forward, as if to read more easily.

After a few seconds it occurred to me to wonder how come he was tipping so far. He had been leaning a little bit against my new reading lamp.

I pulled the washcloth away from my eyes. There was no reading lamp.

It was a really nice one that Mom had gotten me at a thrift store to go with my new color scheme. It had, she said, been pretty expensive to begin with, and the people at the shop hadn't realized it could have been sold as an antique, because she'd only paid five dollars for it. It had a shade big enough to let me use a decent-sized lightbulb in it, and it was positioned right alongside my bed so I could read with it. Reading after Jodie wanted to go to sleep was one of the most important benefits of having a room of my own.

I stared at the empty spot where the lamp was supposed to be.

There was nothing but Oscar, reading his book, his wire-rimmed glasses sliding off the end of his stubby nose.

Anger flared, and I forgot about bathing my eyes with a cool washcloth. Had Jodie borrowed the lamp for some reason and not bothered to bring it back?

I got up and headed for her room.

There it was, neat and silent with all its pink-and-white-checked ruffles, stuffed animals lining the shelves, all in precise positions, just the way my sister kept everything.

There was no sign of my lamp, only Jodie's fussy little pink ones that didn't provide enough light to read or take a sliver out of your finger.

Wally's was the next closest room, so I checked that. We hadn't been in the house long enough for it to be looking the way his room usually looked. There was his bat leaning against one wall, his sweater thrown on the bed (unmade, at least that was normal) and two dishes with the remains of his last ice-cream feast sitting on the floor beside his bed.

No antique reading lamp.

Puzzled, I went on to Jeff's room.

He wasn't a neatnik like Jodie, or a slob like

Wally. I wasn't yet used to the way his new room was supposed to look, so I stood in the doorway, surveying the place. There was no sign of my lamp, but something didn't seem quite right. I decided to stand there until I figured it out.

He had stacks of sheet music on his desk, a couple of books on music theory, and a biography of Joseph Haydn, which anchored the sheet music.

After a few more seconds I saw that something was missing from here, too. Jeff had a nice radio-CD player, which he kept right next to his bed on a nightstand. It wasn't there.

What the heck was going on?

By this time, I was really puzzled. I crossed the hall to the master bedroom, where Mom hadn't added anything new to the furnishings. But in spite of the familiar bedspread and chest of drawers, it all seemed strange in the unfamiliar surroundings.

Finally I realized that not everything was present here, either.

The radio-telephone Dad kept on his side of the bed was missing. The black velvet chest that held Mom's jewelry wasn't on the dresser. She didn't have any real jewelry; the only diamond she owned was in her engagement ring, and she was wearing that. But there were earrings and a few necklaces and a nice string of artificial pearls, all in the velvet box that had held them for as long as I could remember.

And Dad had an elegant pair of gold cuff links that he wore on special occasions in French cuffs, when he was super dressed up. He'd kept them in a little brass tray, with a tiepin and some other small items I couldn't remember. The tray was there, but the cuff links were gone.

The nasal spray was clearing up my allergy problems, and my head was beginning to clear out as well.

Something strange was going on, and I couldn't imagine what it was.

I stepped to the door of Mom and Dad's bathroom and saw that the medicine cabinet door was open, and a couple of prescription bottles had fallen into one of the twin sinks. We didn't use much in the way of pills or remedies for small illnesses, so the rest of the stuff was still there: shaving cream, deodorant, shampoo, mousse.

I think it was right about then that the hairs started to stand up on the back of my neck. Somebody—not the family—had been in our house since we'd left that morning.

I turned back into my parents' bedroom, looking for the phone. I'd call Mom. She was more likely to be where I could reach her immediately than Dad was. He had to be out and moving around the high school most of the time.

But there was no phone. It had been unplugged from the wall and taken away.

My heart began to beat more loudly, so I could hear it in my ears, and there was a strange, frightened feeling creeping over me like bugs on a dead squirrel.

Downstairs, I heard a door close. For a few seconds I didn't think I could breathe or move. I forgot I'd just had an allergy attack and that now I was supposed to go back to school. I forgot everything except that I was alone in the house with someone who had no right to be there.

# five

I felt as if I couldn't catch my breath, and my chest hurt.

I listened, hearing nothing more in the house. There shouldn't have been any noises, because except for me the place was supposed to be empty. But I was sure I'd heard a door close downstairs. And the front door had been unlocked! How had that happened? An accident?

Maybe Mom had remembered leaving the door unlocked, or maybe she'd finished whatever she'd been in the middle of at the clinic and had come home to check on me, just in case. Maybe she had opened and closed a door.

But Mom would have called out for me immediately when she came in.

I stood there, frozen, beginning to ache with the effort of holding myself so still. And as my gaze drifted around my parents' bedroom, I remembered the things that were missing: my lamp, Jeff's radio, Mom's jewelry box, and Dad's gold cuff links.

I remembered the Andersons' house, where three men had stolen a whole lot of stuff and vanished with it before the police could get there. I remembered that one of them had hit Jeff over the head and knocked him out.

The hairs prickled on the top of my head.

I couldn't call the police. The telephone had been unplugged and carried away.

I finally sucked in a great gulp of air and made myself move, slowly and cautiously, toward a window looking out over Mrs. Banducci's house. For once she wasn't out there spraying water on the street as an excuse to see what the neighbors were doing.

Actually, there probably weren't any neighbors around this time of day. This was a new subdivision, with expensive houses that probably took two people working in every family to pay for them. Like ours. If I could have seen anyone, I'd have opened the window and yelled.

I felt cold, although it was ordinary early fall weather, no hint of chill when I'd walked home from school.

What should I do?

There were two other phones in the house, one in the living room and one in the kitchen. Unless, of course, someone had unplugged those, too. They were my best chance to get help.

Maybe, since the thieves had obviously already been up here and taken the things that looked the most interesting, it would be safe just to wait here until they'd cleaned out what they wanted and left the house.

My aunt Jane had brought us all wristbands the last time she came to visit. They were different colors of leather—brown for Wally (appropriately dirt colored, Jeff had pointed out), black for Jeff, blue for me, and pink, of course, for Jodie. They had gold letters stamped on each of them—WWJD? The letters stood for "What Would Jesus Do?" and wearing them was supposed to remind you to reflect on your choices before it was too late.

It was easy enough to figure out what Jesus would do in most situations. The right thing, the kind thing, the loving thing.

But those choices didn't apply here.

The question was, what would Dad advise me to do? Call the police, if it were possible. But since it wasn't, unless I went downstairs and found a working phone, would he want me to hide up here until the housebreakers were gone?

The Andersons had lost a whole lot of stuff—a computer, TVs, the family silver—and so far they hadn't retrieved any of it. I didn't even know if all of our things were insured, except for Jeff's piano. I knew nobody had carried off the piano, at least not yet. I had noticed it when I looked at those mysterious boxes downstairs.

That didn't mean the strangers wouldn't come back and get it, even if it was hard to move, because it was very valuable. And thinking of valuable, I tried to recall if the new big-screen TV had still been in the corner of the living room.

I hadn't noticed. We hadn't had it very long. Would it be included on our old home owners' insurance, or would Dad have had to especially put it on the policy?

In spite of what Mom had said about how economically feasible this new house was, I knew the family budget had been strained by our move. The money from the sale of the old place had provided the down payment and paid for the new living room set after they decided to put the old one in the family room. But they'd stretched things to cover the big TV and a few other things. Losing anything we owned would be a serious matter. I knew we didn't have the money to replace any of it.

So, what would Dad want me to do?

Suddenly, downstairs, there were voices. Men's voices.

I jumped away from the window, which offered me nothing in the way of help, and tried to think. My parents always told all of us that we were intelligent and capable. If that was the case, why had my brain gone numb? I eased out into the hallway so I could hear better.

"They sure got a million books in this place," somebody muttered. "They're in just about every room. We gonna take any of those?"

"Nah. Books aren't worth anything. Get that set of candlesticks off the mantle. I think maybe they're silver."

"We gonna take that picture of the mountain?" one of the men asked clearly.

I knew the picture they were talking about. It was of Mount Baker, in northern Washington, where Mom and Dad had met years ago on a hiking trip. It had been Mom's first climb, and Dad had rescued her when she'd fallen into a snow-filled gully.

"It was love at first sight," Dad had told us. "There she was, floundering around helplessly in a snowbank, with only a bright red knitted cap sticking out."

"And he had enough muscle to pull me out, one-handed, and he shared a Thermos of hot coffee," Mom always added when they told the story.

Mom had bought him the picture as a birthday present, and I knew he really liked it.

I felt a sudden rush of rage at the way these strangers had invaded our home and were helping themselves to our belongings.

How could I stop them, without access to a telephone?

Was there a way to get out of the house without being detected? I could run to a neighbor's house to call the police before they got away. Well, Mrs. Banducci's house was undoubtedly the only one where there was anyone home, but she'd call in a minute, I was sure.

The trouble was, I was on the second floor, and the only stairway down would take me to where the thieves were. Dad had talked about getting one of those emergency ladders to hang out a window—in fact, he'd even ordered one, but it hadn't come yet. I was way too high up to risk jumping; I'd break bones for sure.

There was no roof to crawl out on, and the idea made me queasy, anyway. Jodie, with her dance training, wasn't afraid to balance on anything a couple of inches wide. Me, I was the family klutz. I could fall off a sidewalk.

I moved as silently as I could around to all the

rooms on the top floor, checking to make sure I wasn't overlooking any means of escape. There was nothing, and in the meantime I was hearing voices from downstairs and the scrape of something heavy across a bare wood floor.

In the end I had to give up on getting out of the house from the second floor. I hesitated in the upper hallway, out of sight of anyone from below, listening.

"Hey, look! In this cabinet here. You think this would be worth anything?"

"A chess set? I dunno. It's just wood, isn't it?"

"Yeah. But I think it's hand carved, and old. Maybe an antique."

Grandpa's chess set, I thought, the outrage flooding through me anew. The one Dad's grandfather had made from some kind of rare wood, many years ago. It was one of my father's prized possessions. I remembered how upset he'd gotten when he'd come home one day and found Wally and one of his friends playing with it on the floor. It would be a lot worse if these thieves took it.

"It's probably one of a kind. Might be too easy to trace," the deeper of the two voices answered. "Maybe we'd better forget that. What do you think about that piano, though?"

For a few seconds I didn't hear what they said next. I saw red as my vision blurred.

Not Jeff's piano! He'd be heartbroken if he

lost his piano, even if it was insured! It would be like losing his child. No amount of money could compensate for losing this one, no matter what replaced it.

I had to find a way to stop them.

"It's gonna be the devil to load," the higher voice grumbled. "I don't care if it is worth thousands. And we'd have to be careful. Nobody's gonna pay big money for a piano if it's scratched, so we'd have to wrap it in blankets or something. . . ."

"Plenty of bedding upstairs. Let's take it. It could bring more than all the rest of it put together."

"Let's quit yapping and get moving. We ain't got all day. Buddy'll be back with the truck in a few minutes, and who knows how long that nosy old biddy will be busy with her flooded garage? Let's go."

Not with Jeff's piano, I thought. I'd have to sneak past them, somehow, and out the back door, maybe. I couldn't just hide up here until they went away. Not if they were stealing Dad's mountain picture and the piano. No amount of insurance would make up for their loss, not to Dad or Jeff.

There hadn't been a truck in sight to haul things in when I'd entered the house. I was confused and frantic; I had to calm down enough to be logical, somehow.

They couldn't haul away anything like the piano unless they had a good-sized vehicle. I tried to remember what I'd heard them saying to each other. There had been a truck. Hadn't Mrs. Banducci said there was a delivery truck earlier? Yes, she'd wanted to know what we were having delivered, and I'd said I didn't know.

Of course they hadn't been delivering anything, except maybe those empty cardboard boxes. And then, for some reason, one of them had left with the truck. And . . . I dredged it up through my frightened memory. One of them had said, "Buddy'll be back with the truck in a few minutes."

How long did I have? They'd mentioned Mrs. Banducci, too, I supposed. They'd called her a "nosy old biddy," and who else could that be? Somehow they'd managed to flood her garage, and she was presumably next door cleaning up a mess, a project to keep her and her curiosity out of the way while they did what they'd come to do.

There was no time to waste. I had to get out of the house, run next door, and call 911, and then my dad, before it was too late. There was only one main street coming into Lofty Cedars Estates. If the police could get to the entrance to this subdivision, they could cut them off; there was no other way to escape.

Sometimes when I get overexcited, Dad will tell me, "Calm down, Kaci. Stand still and take a couple of deep breaths. It'll make your brain work better."

I tried it. It felt like drawing in deep breaths was making a terrible cramp in my chest, but after a moment I had settled down to just mild tremors.

I edged closer to the top of the stairs. I could hear their voices—two of them, I decided, and hoped I was right—somewhere in the back of the house. Well, then, I'd run out the front door if I could get to it.

I started to creep down the stairs, glad they were carpeted, so I didn't make any noise. I was halfway down when I heard the engine as a truck pulled into the driveway.

For a few seconds I regressed into total panic. Should I run back upstairs? Hide again? What?

"Hey, I think I hear Buddy." The voice was almost below me, and I swallowed hard and dropped to my hands and knees so they wouldn't see me through the railing if they looked up. I had no choice but to retrace my steps, crawling as fast as I could.

"What took you so long?" the deeper voice said as the front door opened.

If the truck driver had looked up instead of

straight ahead, he'd have seen me for sure. I reached the landing and went flat, praying hard that they wouldn't notice me. I remembered I was still wearing that bright red backpack and I squirmed forward on my stomach, working my way around the corner. I was sweating and I felt the trickle of moisture working its way down my face.

"I'm only ten minutes later than I said I'd be," Buddy stated. "You guys get those boxes filled up so we can start moving them out of here. We ought to get out of this place before anybody comes home and catches us."

"Except for the old witch next door, the whole neighborhood is empty." That was the one who thought the piano was too heavy to move. "I hope she didn't have sense enough to call a plumber."

"I told you, I cut her phone wire. She can't call anybody. It's not likely she's got a cell phone, old broad like her."

Cell phone. I swallowed hard. Dad and Mom had a cell phone they carried when they were out late at night, or other times when they thought they might need it. When it wasn't in use, it was left on the desk in the study.

My hope died quickly, though. The thieves had probably already been in there and cleaned out everything of any value. If they'd taken all the other phones, they'd probably swept that one up, too.

Knowing that I couldn't call from next door was a bummer. What was the next best thing to do? Would I be in terrible trouble if I ran to one of the other houses and smashed a window to get in to reach a phone that was still working?

I wondered if that was how the men had gotten into our house. Around in back, maybe, where they'd be out of sight if anyone came along, had they broken a window and then opened up the front door from inside?

It didn't matter. What mattered was that I had to get out of there as soon as possible. But I couldn't do anything as long as the three men were in the lower hallway.

They were wrangling now about the piano. Buddy, too, thought it was too heavy to move. The deep-voiced one, who seemed to be the leader, was emphatic. "I'm telling you guys, those things are worth a lot of money. It'll be worth the effort. We all work together, we can move it. That's why we got a truck with a lift on it."

"Well, whatever we're gonna do, let's get at it. I don't like working in a cul-de-sac like this place. If you want the confounded piano, let's get it loaded. It's gonna be hard to hide until we can unload it, though."

"We gotta wrap it up, remember? So it won't get scratched. Nobody's gonna pay big bucks for one that has scratches on it."

"So get some blankets or something," the deep, surly voice responded.

Blankets. All the bedrooms were up here. I was around the corner from them, so I quickly stood up and headed for the nearest open doorway. No, not a bedroom, this was where they'd come. Unless I hid in a closet.

I ducked into Mom and Dad's room, running across the carpet and sliding open the mirrored doors. They made a little sound as I squeezed inside and closed them behind me, praying again. Please, God. Please, don't let them catch me, or hear me. I was wheezing as if I'd been running hard.

I wouldn't even have been able to hear the thief enter the room if he hadn't been grumbling about being the one sent to fetch the blankets.

I waited after the grumbling stopped, wondering if it was safe to come out yet. Finally, very slowly, I slid open the door and emerged. The man had stripped the spread off the bed and the blanket that had been under it, leaving sheets trailing on the floor.

Forcing myself to breathe slowly and as normally as possible, I made my way out into the hall.

I turned toward the stairs, hoping they'd all go outside at the same time to load things, so I could run for the kitchen door into the backyard.

The voice behind me was unexpected, as was the rough hand that slammed me against a wall, bruising my arm.

"Hey, guys," the voice said, "we got a little problem up here."

# six

He was big. Over six feet, and thick through the chest and neck. The hand that gripped my arm was huge and rough. His dark hair was longish and didn't look as if he'd washed it recently, and there was a smell about him of sweat and tobacco.

He yelled to his conspirators downstairs. "Hey, guys! Come up here! We got a problem!" he informed them again.

"So take care of it," the leader shouted back.

For a few seconds I stared into those dark eyes, wondering if I'd faint in terror at what I saw there. I started to sag, and he slammed me against the wall for the second time.

"You want me to kill her, or what?" my captor demanded loudly.

There was a startled silence, and then both of the other men appeared at the bottom of the stairs. "Her?" one of them echoed. "What the . . . ?"

I'd never heard some of the words that came out of their mouths, but I didn't have any difficulty interpreting them as profanity.

They stared at me in disbelief.

"There wasn't supposed to be anybody here," the leader said. "What are you doing here, kid?"

It was a wonder I could speak, my mouth was so dry. "I . . .I live here," I stammered.

I could see them evaluating that, and the expressions on their faces were unnerving, to say the least. "You want me to kill her, or what?" Had he been serious when he'd asked that?

"How long you been here?" the leader demanded.

I swallowed hard, and my throat worked, but I couldn't speak as cold terror worked its way down my body, making me weak all over. I didn't even know the answer to his question. Had I been home for an hour, ten minutes, what? I couldn't tell.

The one holding my arm gave me a shake, his big fingers pressing painfully into my arm. "How long?" he asked harshly.

My lips trembled, but nothing came out of

them. I'd prayed only a few minutes ago, but now I was too numb even to do that.

"She couldn't have called the cops. The phones are all gone. I put 'em in a box with the other little junk that I carried away in the first load."

"So who knows you're here?" the deeper-voiced leader asked. He was standing a few steps below me, now, and his eyes, a very pale blue, were boring into mine. Blue eyes ought to have been friendly, but these weren't. They were icy, mean.

I tried once more to speak. What would they do if they thought someone else knew and would rescue me very soon?

"My school nurse knows," I managed to croak desperately. "And my mom. She's . . . supposed to pick me up in a few minutes. . . ."

They were communicating something with their eyes. I couldn't read them for sure, but I didn't think they believed me.

"She's lying," my closest tormentor said. "Nobody's coming to get her."

The leader licked his lips, glaring as if he really was ready to strangle me with his bare hands, right there in the upstairs hall. "Well, we don't want to take any chances. Let's get the rest of the stuff loaded and get out of here."

"What are we gonna do with her, then?"

"Tie her up. It'll take all three of us to load that piano. The rest of the stuff won't take long, but let's move it. Just in case somebody does show up."

I wasn't prepared to be shoved suddenly forward onto the stairs. I went down on one knee and was jerked upward as if my captor didn't care how much he hurt me getting me where he wanted me to go. "Buddy, get me some of that clothesline we're gonna use to keep the blankets on the piano." He was propelling me down the stairs, and it took all the effort I had to stay on my feet. If I fell he'd probably drag me or walk on me, and I was already hurting from the pressure of his hand. He was strong enough to make me do anything he wanted; there was no point in struggling and getting hurt even worse.

"Where'll I tie her? We're taking all the chairs out of here," he said as we reached the main floor.

Our dining room set was as old as I was, and I didn't think it would be worth much if they sold it, but it was the only one we had. I was sagging again, but the man held me up with one hand, as if it were no effort at all.

"We're not taking the kitchen chairs," the leader said. "They're just junk."

Under other circumstances I'd have been insulted to hear our possessions described as junk. Right this minute I was too scared to care.

"Hurry up, Bo," Buddy said, and the one called Bo thrust me ahead of him along the hallway to the back of the house, banging me against the walls as we went.

"It won't do you any good to resist," he told me angrily as he used one foot to pull a chair out from the table and forced me to sit on it. "If you don't behave, don't think I won't hurt you."

I had no doubt about that at all. I collapsed into the chair, glad to sit down, because I wasn't going to be able to stand, anyway. The backpack was a bulky weight between me and the chair, but he didn't take it off.

"Put your hands behind the back of the chair," he ordered. I obeyed, feeling him looping the rope around the crossbars so that even if I stood up I wouldn't be able to free myself of the chair. I wondered frantically if they'd just take our goods and go, leaving me behind. I'd have to sit here until someone came home and found me, and by then they'd be miles away. It no longer seemed to matter so much if they took Dad's picture and Jeff's piano. What mattered was still being alive when my parents came home.

He pulled a wicked-looking knife out of a

scabbard on his belt and cut off a length of clothesline. I yelped when he tightened the rope around my wrists. "It hurts!" I protested, but he didn't loosen it.

"Tough," he said. "Get used to it."

He was close enough to me so I could smell him more than before, an acrid, sour smell of nervous sweat.

"Come on, Bo!" one of the others shouted, and he gave me a threatening look as he wound the rest of the rope around a table leg so it and the chair and I were secured together.

"Don't try anything or you'll get hurt," he threatened before he left me there.

I didn't have any confidence that I wouldn't be hurt no matter how cooperative I was. From where I sat, I could see the broken glass in a window over the sink, confirming my guess about where they'd broken in. The table wasn't heavy; I could have dragged it with me toward the sliding doors onto the rear deck, but then what? I couldn't get loose, and I couldn't get untied to be free of the chair.

For a person who'd read so many adventure stories about people who rescued themselves from dangerous situations, I was doing a terrible job of coming up with any kind of solution to my own mess. The rope was digging into my wrists, and I wondered how quickly the circulation would be cut off enough to do real damage. Tentatively, I tried to slide my chair across the vinyl floor. It made a horrible screeching sound, and I stopped, heart pounding, afraid Bo would hear it and come back.

For a moment or two I heard their voices, and then I figured they'd gone out the front door and were either too far away or were being quiet to avoid attracting attention.

It was very quiet in the house. I tried to control the hammering of my heart, tried again to think clearly. There must be something I could do that would help.

A shadowy movement at the sliding door that opened onto the back deck brought my head around so fast that my neck cracked painfully.

There was a figure out there, small and in a flowered dress. The woman pressed her face against the glass, her hands up on each side so she could peer into the kitchen more easily.

Mrs. Banducci!

I sucked in an excited breath. "Help!" I called out, hoping she could hear me. The sliding door wasn't the glass that was broken, however, and I didn't think I'd caught her attention. It was shadowy in here, and bright sunshine outside, making it hard for her to see into the kitchen.

Then I realized she hadn't seen me. She tried the slider, which of course was still locked. I was afraid to yell any louder for fear of attracting the attention of the thieves. "Run for help!" I urged, unsure of whether or not my voice could reach her.

The old lady pulled back from the glass with a scowl on her face and turned away with no indication that she'd spotted me there, tied to a chair. I didn't dare yell any louder. I could hear the men coming through the house. I could even make out their words.

"What are we going to do with that kid?" one of them asked. "She's seen our faces. She can describe us to the cops."

I shook my head at Mrs. Banducci, hoping the movement would make it easier to see me. "Run!" I said, but softly because I didn't want them to hear me. "Get help!" But I knew she didn't hear me or see me, either one.

She withdrew from the sliding-glass doors and disappeared, leaving me ready to fly apart in all directions.

The voices were coming nearer. "Are we going to have to shut her up permanently?"

My throat closed, and I was begging silently, *Please, God, please God, let her have seen me! Let her get to a phone!*

"Nobody has a gun," the reply came, just

outside the kitchen door. "How you want to do it? Drown her in a bathtub? Burn the house down around her?"

I'd been gasping for breath. Now I stopped breathing at all.

"Starting a fire's the quickest way to get somebody here in a hurry. There may not be anyone left in the subdivision, but there are plenty of people only a few blocks away who would report smoke."

"So what do we do, then? Strangle her with our bare hands? You want me to do it?"

I forgot my wrists were hurting. How quickly could Mrs. Banducci locate a phone? Would she be in time? And all the time I was thinking, she didn't even see me.

My chest was burning, and I finally thought to take a gulp of air before my lungs burst. They were here now, two of them, staring at me as if I were a pig they were about to butcher, and with no more emotion than if that were the case.

"We'd better ask Cal," Buddy said, and now I knew all their names, or at least their nicknames. For all the good it was going to do me. They weren't planning to give me a chance to tell anybody.

"Where'd he go?" Bo asked, turning to look behind him.

"I don't know. He was right behind us." Buddy was studying me in a way that made my skin crawl.

"Well, we've already been here longer than we expected to be. If we want to get this stuff unloaded and get back to another house yet today, we've gotta move."

The one called Buddy wiped his arm across his mouth. "This place may be full of good houses, but it's beginning to spook me. We weren't supposed to run into anybody during the day, and I don't like it. Cal said there wouldn't be anybody in the whole subdivision." He continued to glare at me as if I'd deliberately upset their plans and deserved to be punished for it.

Far off in the distance, we all heard the sudden wail of a siren.

Hope leaped in my chest. Had Mrs. Banducci managed to get to a phone after all? Were the police on the way?

Hope wasn't what I saw on Buddy's and Bo's faces. Consternation instantly turned them from tough guys to cowards.

"Let's get out of here!" Buddy said. "Before it's too late!"

I prayed with all my heart that it was already too late, and then I realized that the siren wasn't getting any louder. It wasn't coming any closer.

Buddy realized it, too. "It's not for us," he said. "It's going away."

At once they turned mean again. For a moment I thought I was going to be stabbed when the knife came out; instead, Bo cut me loose from the chair, with my hands still tied behind me. He jerked me to my feet, wrenching my shoulder so that I cried out involuntarily.

"Shut up," he told me gruffly, and shoved me ahead of him toward the front of the house.

"Cal, where you been? What're we gonna do with this kid?"

Cal looked as if somebody had just stomped on his big toe. "We gotta fix a flat before we can get out of here."

Shock was etched on the other two faces. "It was okay when I drove in here," Buddy asserted. "You sure?"

Cal practically snarled, "You think I can't tell when a tire goes flat? You're the idiots who stole the truck, you get out there and fix it while I finish up in here."

"There is a spare, right?" Bo asked. "And a jack? Okay, we'll get it fixed. I don't know about you guys, but I want out of this place. I'm not sure I even want to come back for the next house, after finding this kid in here. There might be somebody home in the other places, too. You gonna take care of her?"

Bo headed out the front door, but Buddy still stood there, glowering. "We gonna have to kill her? I didn't sign up for no murder, you know. Stealing's something else. They don't put you in prison for life or execute you for taking a truckload of furniture. They probably wouldn't even catch us for that. But killing a kid . . ." He swore again. "They'd never stop looking for us if we kill her."

I was wilting with fear; only his brutal hand kept me from falling. I was dizzy and sick to my stomach, yet if I keeled over he might finish me off right that minute.

"No, we're not gonna kill her," Cal said. He was looking right at me, but his countenance was no friendlier than it had been earlier. I was not misled into being reassured.

It was a wonder that my eyes could even track at that point, but suddenly I caught a flicker of movement behind Cal, through the dining room window.

Mrs. Banducci again!

Her face was pressed to the glass, with her hands shielding her eyes from the sides as she tried once more to see into the interior of the house.

I must have reacted, though I tried not to, because Cal and Buddy both twitched and turned toward the window. They both cursed at the same time. I didn't know whether Bo meant to slam me against the wall again or not, but the pain that shot through my elbow made me go blind and numb for a few seconds.

"It's that old witch next door," Cal said thickly. "I thought one of you was gonna check and make sure she was still up to her behind in the water you turned loose in her garage. Go after her! Don't let her get to a phone to call the cops! I'll take care of this one!"

I slid down the wall when Bo let go of me, curling forward as my head got banged, too. I felt the tears seeping out of my eyes and couldn't get my hands free to wipe at them or rub my elbow. My nose was starting to run disgustingly, and I couldn't do anything about that, either.

Cal looked down on me contemptuously. "This should have been a good gig, but you and that stupid old woman have spoiled it all. We'll be gone as soon as they get that spare tire on. I've got a few more things to throw in this last box, and then we're out of here. And if you try to move while I'm doing that, you'll be sorry, sister."

I wished I could tell him what I thought of him, but even if I could have found enough voice to do it, I was afraid of him. From where I was sprawled on the floor, I could see those size twelve combat boots and I imagined them kicking into me while I lay helpless.

He turned his back on me, confident that he'd cowed me into submission. I could see him through the archway between the dining room and the living room, tossing things carelessly into the last of the cardboard cartons. He was even including the embroidered pillows that Aunt Kathie had given Mom for her last birthday. As I watched through a blur of tears, he took down the full-length mirror that hung just inside the front door so people could check their appearance at the last minute as they left the house.

My tears had initially been because of pain, but they were gradually encompassing another kind of suffering. I knew Mom was going to be devastated when she saw all the things missing from her wonderful new house.

And when I thought about it a moment longer, I realized she and Dad and even Jeff and Jodie and Wally most likely would grieve for me, too.

Cal had said they weren't going to kill me, but did that mean not right now, or never? I had a dismal conviction that I'd be lucky if I ever saw any of my family again.

It hurt to be in the position I was in, with my hands still tied behind me, twisting sideways. I tried to shift, hoping to ease a cramp in my ribs. Something small fell out of the backpack onto the hardwood floor of the dining room, rolling under me.

Cal immediately paused in the act of picking up the box he'd finally filled and gave me a suspicious look.

I swiveled my head around and wiped my nose on the shoulder of my T-shirt. Gross, but preferable to letting it run down into my mouth.

"Stay put," Cal said in a hard voice, and carried the box out and loaded it into the yawning back of the truck. He slammed the double doors shut and secured them with a bar, then walked up to the side of the truck to where Buddy was almost finished with replacing the flat tire.

I could see the license plate quite clearly. VCT 7258. I wondered if I could memorize it, and then remembered that I wasn't going to be around long enough to relay it to the police.

Whatever had fallen out of an outer pocket of the backpack and rolled under me was hard, unyielding. I tried to shift my position again to get off from it, and saw a pencil. A nice new number 2 yellow pencil, with a sharpened point.

It would write the truck's license number, I thought, heart quickening. If the men stayed away long enough. If I could find anything to write on quickly enough.

There was nothing but a smooth, freshly painted white wall beside me.

Pain shot through my arms when I pushed into a sitting position and scrabbled behind me for the pencil. I had to ignore pain, I told myself. This was life or death, and I didn't have to remind myself whose death it would be, or how quickly it might come.

Cal was still talking to his cohort beside the truck, neither of them looking toward me. My heart pounding, my breath coming in gasps, I maneuvered around so my back was to the wall, the pencil awkwardly gripped in my right hand even though my elbow was still throbbing.

I tried to figure out how to write so it would be right side up, and couldn't. My mind was racing so hard, it was a miracle I could think with any logic at all. Okay, write it upside down. If anyone saw it, they'd be able to make sense of it, anyway. I hoped.

Behind me I felt the sharp point break off the pencil lead. I was pushing too hard. I was suffocating, as if someone had put a bag over my head and cut off my air. I tried again to write, hoping that not all the lead had snapped.

"Take your hands off me, you ruffian!"

The screeching female voice made me jerk on the last number. I'd probably left a trailing mark up the wall; I couldn't see it without squirming into a different position, and with the men outside in plain sight, I didn't dare try. I couldn't do anything about it, anyhow.

Mrs. Banducci, her hair wildly disarranged, came into view with Bo propelling her. She was kicking backward, and she connected with one of his shins, so that he yelped and called her an unprintable name. "Cut it out before I have to really hurt you," he told her, giving her a shake that knocked her glasses askew.

"What do you want me to do with her?" he demanded in exasperation. "Stick her in the back of the truck, or do we have to dispose of her, too?"

I didn't miss that "too." I pushed the pencil behind me up against the baseboard, afraid that it would show up, bright yellow against white, when I had to be moved. There was nothing else I could do about that.

"Yeah," Cal said. "And stay back there with her."

Bo scowled. "Hey, why do I have to be in the back where I can't see what's going on?"

"Because," Cal said, angry at being challenged, "there's only room for three of us in the front."

"So since when am I not one of the three of us?" Bo was getting mad, too.

"Since we need to keep the kid up front," Cal told him. "She's no use as a hostage if we can't get at her if the cops stop us. Come on, the tire's fixed, let's get on the road."

He was so furious that when he reentered the house and jerked me to my feet, he didn't see the pencil against the baseboard, or the message I'd written on the wall above it.

He dragged me out the front door, shut it behind us, and hauled me up into the front of the truck. Buddy got into the driver's seat, Cal squeezed himself against my right side, and Buddy turned on the ignition.

*Hostage.*

The word echoed in my mind as the truck began to move.

I was a hostage. I crumpled inwardly and was unable to stop the tears that welled up, blurring my vision.

That meant that if they had a confrontation with the police, they'd hold me up in front of someone so the officers couldn't fire at them.

It was about as terrifying a situation as you could get.

# seven

I didn't know whether to hope the police would stop us going out of Lofty Cedars Estates or not.

I'd seen lots of movies where hostages were held in front of gunmen so the cops didn't dare to shoot for fear of hitting the victim. Yet I knew that the farther we got from the scene of the crime, the poorer my chances were of escaping alive.

And poor Mrs. Banducci, what about her? She was undoubtedly as much at risk as I was. She, too, had had a good look at them and could identify them. Once they were sure they'd gotten away with their thefts and unloaded their loot, would they see any reason to let either the old lady or me stay alive?

I'd scribbled the license number on a wall, but the chances of anyone coming home and finding it before the end of the school day were practically nil. Wally usually had some kind of practice when he got out, and if there was a day when he didn't, he went to day care until it was time for the rest of us to get home. Jodie, at ten, was allowed to come home alone, as long as she checked in with Mom at the clinic. She wasn't allowed to have other kids over unless one of our parents was there. She had a few chores to do when she was home alone. She was more likely to check in with Mom to see if she could go to someone else's house for a few hours, as long as it was okay with her friend's mother, who was expected to be present.

Jeff, then, would usually be the first one to get home, and that wouldn't be for hours yet. He'd know the minute he walked in that the place had been robbed; he'd call Dad, and then the police, but who knew how long it would be before anyone noticed my scribble on the wall?

It didn't seem likely that this scenario was going to play out in a promising way. I wondered what time it was. Noon, at least, surely. My stomach rumbled the way it does when I don't eat at the time I'm used to. I was supposed to check in with the nurse when I got back to school. Would

Mrs. Burton notice that I hadn't come back after going home for my allergy spray? Would she call Mom if she did remember? And what would Mom do? Come looking for me, or just assume that I was on my way?

Actually, Mom wasn't much for assuming that everything was all right without checking on us. Usually it was annoying, because we'd only forgotten to call, or gotten held up for some innocent reason.

Today, I prayed she'd check. In person. And bring in the police.

We eased out of the driveway and drove slowly toward the exit from the subdivision without a sign of a police car and not very many pedestrians and private cars. Nobody paid any attention to us.

I heard Cal's exhalation of relief as we turned onto a main street that led to the freeway. And after a minute or so I noticed that Buddy's white-knuckled grip on the steering wheel had loosened a little bit.

Did it make it better or worse that he was less nervous?

"I hope this bucket of rust holds together until we can get rid of it," Buddy commented, shifting gears with an effort. "It wouldn't surprise me if it fell apart before we get it unloaded."

"You're the one who picked it out," Cal told him unsympathetically. "I said an older truck that wasn't likely to be noticed, not one that had over two hundred thousand miles on it and looked like nobody ever changed the oil."

At the mention of the mileage, I glanced down and spotted the figures on the odometer. Two hundred thousand and forty-two miles. Maybe, I thought hopefully, it would break down before we reached our destination and they'd have to abandon it, leaving me with it. It wasn't likely, but it seemed a better thing to imagine than any of the alternatives that came to mind.

In stories, the heroine takes advantage of a time when the criminals are off guard. I doubted that either of them was really relaxing yet—they still had a whole load of stolen goods—but I couldn't think of anything feasible to try even if they both went completely limp. I knew from having been jerked around that they were strong enough to hurt me. By tomorrow—if I were still alive tomorrow—I knew there would be bruises.

I still had my hands tied behind me, and the bulky backpack supported me above my hands. It was horribly uncomfortable. I squirmed a little, flinching because this brought me up against Cal, but I couldn't stand the strained position without trying to ease it.

Cal gave me a sour look, without comment. He must have known how I felt, but he didn't offer to do anything about it.

A blue and white police car pulled out in front of us.

Buddy jerked and hit the brakes, throwing me forward, almost off the seat.

"Be careful!" Cal said sharply. "I thought you could drive this thing!"

Buddy snapped back. "You think you can do any better, I'll pull over and give you a chance to try it. What did you want me to do, plow into the back of the cops and get asked for the papers on this wreck?"

I was staring hungrily at the police car, only a few tantalizing yards away. Was there any way I could get their attention?

Cal had glanced at me and must have read my thoughts. "Don't get any ideas, kid," he said. And then, to Buddy, "Where's that duct tape we had?"

"I threw it under the seat," Buddy said, still seething over the aspersions cast on his driving ability.

Cal leaned over and fished around, then withdrew a roll of the silvery tape people use to mend everything from broken windows to split pipes. I looked at it uncomprehendingly until Cal tore off a strip, twisted around, and plastered it over my eyes.

I yelped a protest before I could stop it, jerking away from him, which threw me against Buddy. He, in turn, swore his own objections, but Cal was pressing the tape down firmly, right into my hair on both sides, leaving me blind.

"Shut up, or I'll plaster your mouth shut, too," Cal warned.

I choked, swallowing, gasping for breath.

I could still breathe, but with my vision cut off, I felt as if I'd die of suffocation if he covered my mouth, too. Tears sprang to my eyes, and I struggled to control them. I didn't think there was any way for them even to run off.

I couldn't see the police car anymore, or anything else. Hope, not very strong to begin with, sank another notch. In the dark, determined not to make things worse by crying, I sat numbly, trying to pray. It wasn't likely anything or anyone else could save me.

I knew when we swerved onto the freeway, turning to the right, throwing me against Cal. There was traffic around us—big trucks, by the sound of them. Once again I heard a siren, one of those ringing up and then down, like the ones they use on ambulances. Not a police car, I guessed, when Buddy kept an even speed. Obviously it didn't spook him, which meant no one was going to stop them or save me.

It was hard to judge how long we rode. Cal

and Buddy didn't talk to each other, or to me. I wanted a drink in the worst way, and I needed to go to the bathroom. My nose was running again, and I wished I had my nasal spray, though this time my problem was probably not due to an allergy. My nose always runs when I cry.

They say when you lose one of your senses, your other senses become more acute. I didn't know if that is true or not, but I concentrated on figuring out which way we were going. I wasn't sure what good it would do to know, but I did it just in case it might be helpful. It gave me something useful to think about.

A right turn onto the freeway, going south. Quite a few miles, and then another turn, and down an off-ramp, then climbing perceptibly. A stop. Traffic going by, then a left turn.

We'd gone off the freeway, over an overpass heading east. A few miles going straight, and less traffic. I didn't hear any eighteen-wheelers, and I guessed we were on a secondary road. Getting close to our destination? Closer to the time when they'd have to decide what to do with me—and Mrs. Banducci—if they decided they no longer needed us for hostages?

In stories and movies, if the hostages are the good guys, they usually get rescued or manage to escape. Unfortunately, a writer who likes happy endings wasn't writing this script. Cal and Buddy and Bo didn't care about happy endings, I was pretty sure. At least not for anyone but themselves.

We made another turn, this one to the left. The sound of the tires on the road surface was different. A gravel road, maybe, instead of pavement?

My heartbeat was speeding up, and I could hear my own breathing, as if I'd been running. Oh, if only I could run!

When Buddy braked without warning, I rocked forward again. Cal stuck out an arm to shove me back against the seat.

We bumped over some rough terrain, and then stopped with a lurch.

"Let's get this stuff unloaded and get rid of this rig," Buddy said, and Cal grunted agreement.

They left me sitting there in the middle of the seat, unable to see, or move my aching arms. It seemed as if they'd been twisted behind me for a long time and my shoulders would pull out of their sockets if someone didn't loosen the rope soon.

I listened to the men's voices, knew they were moving around, opening up the back of the truck, unloading it. I heard the screech of rusting metal—a sliding door being opened? Cursing, something falling with a crash.

"Maybe," Buddy said, so close by the open door that I jumped, "we should leave the piano on the truck and see if that buyer you might have will take a look at it. If he'd take it before we have to handle it again, it would save a lot of muscle."

"No," Cal said bluntly. "It's too risky to haul it around. And we need to get rid of the truck as soon as we can."

"I'll second that," Bo said, also very close. "If that old broad is telling the truth, they'll be looking for us as soon as somebody gets into her house. She says she left a note describing the truck, and that they'll find us any minute. I need to put some of that tape over her mouth."

There was a moment of silence before Cal swore some more. "You think she really did?"

"Who knows? She'd say anything if she thought it would spook us. She could have. But she lives alone, doesn't she? Might be nobody'll go into her house for days."

"Her son sometimes comes on weekends," Bo said.

Had Mrs. Banducci told him that, or did he know that from some other source? Was he one of the neighbors, someone who had information about the people who lived in our new subdivision? Would that make it easier for them to get rid of anyone who might possibly identify them?

"We'd better not take a chance," Cal decided. "Unload everything, including the piano. As soon as it's empty, Buddy can drive the truck off a bridge and dump it where there's a chance nobody'll find it for a while. Maybe we can pick up another one right away and hit one more place yet this afternoon."

"Not in the same area," Buddy said quickly. "We're pushing our luck already in Lofty Cedars."

"No," Cal agreed. "We already cased that Hempstead Lane on the other side of town. That ought to be safer. Come on, let's get the rest of the stuff inside."

Was there a chance someone would see me when they hauled me out of the truck? I wondered. Maybe someone would realize that I was blindfolded and tied—

"Come on, sister," Cal said, practically in my ear. He took hold of my arm and dragged me out of the truck, cracking my head as I stumbled through the doorway. It really hurt, and I sagged down without any way to catch myself. He let me go all the way to the ground, and he swore as I sprawled at his feet, doubling over. He reached past me to get something off the seat, probably the gloves I'd been sitting on

"Take the duct tape off so she can see to walk,"

Buddy growled. "There's nothing she can see here that will matter, is there?"

He didn't even wait for Cal to respond but reached down and ripped off the tape. I yelped again because it felt as if the tape took half my skin and bunches of hair with it, but at least my eyes were uncovered. They were streaming by this time, so that everything around me was blurry.

"Come on, then," Cal said, and pulled me to my feet so roughly that I lost my balance and fell against the edge of the seat I'd just left. I blinked hard and took a few extra seconds, as if to catch my breath, while my gaze swept over the odometer. I could just barely see it.

Two hundred thousand and seventy-nine miles.

We'd driven thirty-seven miles since we'd left home. And we were south and a little bit east of town. I twisted to wipe my face on my shoulder as Cal dragged me upright. I glanced around, trying to see as much as I could in case I got an opportunity to flee.

The nearest building was a barn that looked as if it hadn't been used in a long time. Some distance off to one side stood an apparently abandoned farmhouse, dejected and run-down.

We were way out in the country, with no close

neighbors. So much for my hope that someone would spot me and call for help.

"You'd better just leave us behind and go," Mrs. Banducci's voice said sharply, and I turned my head to see her being pushed ahead of Buddy in our direction. She, too, had her hands tied behind her. "You aren't going to get away with this, but if you left now, you could try to outrun the police. They're after you by this time."

Buddy's irritation seemed mixed with nervousness. After all, she could be telling the truth about having left a message with a description of the truck. He didn't respond to Mrs. Banducci, however, but spoke to Cal.

"We had to get her out of the way so we could unload everything. What do you want me to do with her?"

"For right now, they can both sit here where we can see them." Cal shoved me down onto the ground near the front of the truck. "From what we've seen so far, one of 'em might hot-wire this rig if they get loose. I don't want them to be where they can do anything we won't notice. We'll get rid of them when we're ready to leave."

My eyes met Mrs. Banducci's as she was also pushed onto the ground. She looked more angry than scared. "If you harm us, the sentence will be more severe," she told our captors. "Life in prison. Or execution. We have the death penalty in this state, you know."

"She's getting on my nerves," Buddy said.

"Forget her. Let's just get this stuff off the truck as fast as we can."

They left us there, where they could see us as they worked, and I let out a long breath. I hurt all over. "Do you think they intend to kill us?"

"I really did leave a note on my desk," she informed me. "With a description of the truck. My friend Sarah was coming over for lunch, and when I don't answer the bell, she'll walk in and find the note. The police will be looking for us by this time."

"How will they know where to look, though? We're thirty-seven miles from home, and the police car we passed paid no attention to us."

She considered this, then turned her head to look me over. "You've got a red mark on your forehead, but I hope your brain isn't addled. We've got to think of a way to escape if the police don't get here soon enough."

"We're tied with our hands behind us," I pointed out. "We could get up and run, but I don't think we could outrun them. There's no place to go that isn't right out in the open where they could see us."

Mrs. Banducci pursed her lips, as if that

helped her think better. "Can you reach that little stem thing behind you?"

"Stem thing?" I echoed stupidly.

"On the front tire. It must be almost directly behind you. That's what I used to let the air out of the other tire while the truck was parked in front of your house. If we could make this one go flat, too, they wouldn't be able to move the truck and run it into the river or whatever they were talking about doing. If they can't hide it, the police will find us sooner. They'll put out an APB with my description of it, and somebody will spot it and report it."

"We're way out in the sticks," I said. "Far enough off the main road so it could be a long time before anybody notices it."

"Still, it's in plain sight if anyone drives by." Mrs. Banducci squirmed into a more comfortable position. "We don't have much time. Can you reach that valve thing?"

I wriggled my aching hands and felt for the tire behind me. "Yes, I can feel it. But I don't know if it's a good idea to give them another flat tire. It would make them madder than they already are. That might not be very wise."

"If they're already talking about putting us back in the truck and running it into the river, how much nastier could they get?" the old lady demanded.

My breath caught painfully in my chest. "Is that what they're planning?"

"That Bo and Buddy were talking that way. I don't think the other one—Cal is his name?—has decided, and he's the boss. But he's a mean one, too. So let's give them another flat tire."

"I don't know how to do it," I said. I felt as if I'd fallen into a nightmare and couldn't wake up from it.

"My son told me once how to do it. You have to take the cap off; can you manage that? And then you have to stick something down inside to hold it open while the air leaks out."

"I don't have anything," I told her, feeling less competent by the moment. I glanced toward the rear of the truck, where the men were carrying boxes into the shadowy interior of the barn.

"There's a nail right behind you. I saw it when I sat down. Feel around for it."

Feeling around for anything when your hands are tied behind your back isn't easy. I was sweating and slightly nauseated, but I followed her directions. The cap on the air valve resisted my efforts at first, and then gave way. I found the nail and prayed it wouldn't be too big to fit into the valve in a way to release the air.

When the air whooshed around my fingers, I stifled an exclamation. "It makes so much noise!

They'll hear it!" I almost panicked all over again.

"They're talking and making their own noises. Just let it sit that way until the tire goes flat."

I glanced furtively toward the rear of the truck, where our captors had begun to maneuver Jeff's precious piano onto the lift that would lower it to the ground. They were all grunting and swearing, and as the lift came down it made noises, too.

The escaping air seemed horribly loud in my ears, but the men didn't seem to notice.

"How . . . how long will it take?" I demanded, barely above a whisper.

"I think it took about ten minutes the last time," Mrs. Banducci said. "It seemed like forever, and I wasn't sure they'd stay away long enough for it to work."

My heart sank. "Ten minutes! They'll catch us for sure!"

I imagined one of Buddy's big fists smashing into my face or my stomach, and I flinched. "They'll kill us!"

"At my age, death is something I think about frequently," Mrs. Banducci said. "I know I'm going to Heaven, and that's all right. I just hope it doesn't hurt too much."

"But I'm not even twelve years old yet!" I protested. If she'd expressed her opinion on death sooner, I'm not sure I'd have stuck the nail into the valve to cause a flat tire. "I'm not ready to go to Heaven!"

There was a sudden burst of profanity from where the thieves were struggling to maneuver the grand piano through the barn doorway. I couldn't tell what they were arguing about, but they were definitely disagreeing. I just hoped it kept them occupied while the rest of the air rushed out of the tire behind me. Maybe if they got to fighting among themselves they wouldn't be able to agree on what to do with us. If Mrs. Banducci was right and they intended to lock us in the rear of truck and run it into a river, would a flat tire be enough to foil that idea? Or would they run it, anyway, since they wouldn't care about cutting up a tire?

My stomach muscles suddenly tightened. The men had settled the problem with the baby grand and were stalking purposefully in this direction.

"Don't let them see you're afraid," Mrs. Banducci said, and I wondered how on earth I was supposed to accomplish that when they could probably see my heart pounding beneath my T-shirt.

# eight

The hissing noise behind me had finally ceased.

I stared at the approaching men. My mind was still in too much of a panic to think clearly. I was too numb even to pray except, *Please, God. Please, God.* Usually I can figure out a prayer explaining to God just how to handle a problem, though Grandma said that was pretty presumptuous since the Lord is smart enough to get that part right on His own. This time I hoped that was the case, because I sure didn't have any ideas.

I didn't want to look at their faces, but I couldn't help it. Cal was the leader, and he was the one who would probably make the decision on what to do with us. He looked like a man who could step on us with no more regret than he would have if he crushed a cockroach.

When they got to within about ten feet of us, Buddy asked, "So what do you want to do with these two? We don't need hostages anymore."

"Put them in the back of the truck. Then get rid of it. I'll follow you in the car, and we'll get out of here," Cal said. "Bo, you can ride with me, and Buddy'll take care of the rest of it."

A scowl formed on Buddy's face. "I'm supposed to roll it off into the river, right? So I'll be the one they hang the murder charge on if they catch up with us!"

"They'll hang the murder charge on all three of you if we die," Mrs. Banducci spoke up from where she was sitting on the ground beside the truck. "And they will catch you. At least so far you haven't done anything to get executed for. Why don't you cut your losses and just leave us here?"

I guessed she had watched a lot of crime shows on TV. I didn't know if she was making things better or worse by talking to them that way. She couldn't appeal to their hearts because they didn't seem to have any, if they could so casually talk about disposing of us.

"She's right about one thing," Cal said. "It doesn't matter who actually drives the rig into the water. If they nail one of us, they'll nail all of us. But they won't if we keep our heads. There's nothing to tie us to robbing that house."

"Except I wrote a description of the truck, and they've probably found it by now," Mrs. Banducci said.

Cal gave her a nasty smile. "But we stole the truck, and there's nothing to tie us to that, either. We'll wipe all the fingerprints off the inside of it, for when somebody finds it in the river, and our prints aren't on file anywhere, anyway. Come on, guys, get rolling. We're wasting time."

Buddy still looked uncertain, but I wasn't concerned about Buddy. I didn't know how far he'd try to drive before we and the truck went into the river, but it wouldn't be very long. I've heard that when people are facing death, their entire lives flash before their eyes. All I could think of was that there had to be some way out of this, and I felt frustrated because I couldn't think what it could be. Breathing had become an effort; it was as if I were paralyzed, so I had to concentrate on making the air go in and out, and I felt light-headed and kind of dizzy. I hoped I wasn't going to throw up.

Cal was already striding away toward the house. I hadn't seen a car over there; maybe they'd hidden it back under the trees on the other side so nobody would notice it and wonder why it was there at an abandoned farm.

Buddy, still frowning, reached down and grabbed hold of Mrs. Banducci's thin arm, hauling her to her feet. "Come on, old woman. Back in the truck," he said gruffly.

Bo hesitated. "You want me to bring this one?" he asked about me.

"Yeah, sure." Buddy was being rougher than he needed to be, since he was much bigger and stronger than his victim. Bo wasn't very considerate, either. I felt as if he'd dislocated my shoulder by the time I was on my feet, and my balance was off, so I nearly fell again.

"Look," I managed, "can't you untie our hands? If you're going to lock us in, what difference will it make? We can't do anything to get away, and my nose is running and I can't wipe it, and the rope is too tight! Please—"

Bo didn't even bother to answer. It was a few seconds before I realized why his jaw had first slackened, then tightened in anger. "Buddy! Cal!" he yelled, slamming me against the side of the truck.

"What?" Cal called back, turning around halfway to the house.

"She let the air out of another tire! We got another flat!"

I'd almost forgotten that. I flinched from his angry grip, but I couldn't get away from him. I'd been sitting long enough that my feet were half numb, to match my arms.

There was more swearing as the three of them stood looking at the flat tire.

"How'm I supposed to drive this to the river now?" Buddy demanded, rage sending blood into his face. "Anybody sees us limping along on the rim is going to make us stop. Call the cops, who knows? It's too far to go without a tire, and we used the only spare there was."

"Boy," Bo said sourly, "this is the last time we'll trust you to swipe a vehicle. What a lemon."

Buddy let loose of Mrs. Banducci so fast, she fell against the side of the truck. He took a step toward his cohort with a fisted left hand ready to punch. "It didn't have flat tires when I stole it, stupid! She let the air out of it, see, the valve cap's there on the ground! It couldn't have come off by itself! I'll bet one of them did the same thing with the first tire, back at the house."

He glared at me. For once Mrs. Banducci held her tongue, maybe because she was finally afraid that they might physically hurt us since they were so upset.

My mouth was dry, but I managed to swallow so my throat didn't quite close up.

Cal had the biggest vocabulary of profanity I'd ever heard. He kicked at the offensive flat tire. When he finally pulled himself together, he spoke through clenched teeth. "All right. We'll have to leave it here. We can't pull it into the barn without moving all that furniture, and we can't risk taking the time for that. You can drive it flat as far as where we left the car. It won't be quite so noticeable back there under the trees. Put them in the back of it, and let's get going."

Buddy hesitated. "We gonna leave them alive? So they can describe us if anyone finds 'em?"

The constriction in my chest really hurt. I glanced toward Mrs. Banducci, who was looking as if she might have a heart attack. She was, after all, pretty old and she'd been treated roughly for a long time now. On the other hand, I thought, maybe having a heart attack would be an easier way to go than locked into a truck that was slowly sinking into a river.

I was convinced that for a matter of seconds Cal seriously considered murdering us in cold blood right where we stood.

And then Mrs. Banducci spoke. If she was terrified and shaky, it didn't show. "The cops are busy looking for you," she told them. "Whatever you're going to do, you'd better hurry up or it will be too late."

I closed my eyes for a blissful moment of not seeing those three enraged faces. Did she really want them to hurry up and do something, when the something was eliminating us?

When I opened my eyes again, Cal still looked as if he could chew razor blades. "She's right. We have to move. Put them in the back, drive the truck into the place where I have the car now, and we'll go."

"Leave them alive?" Buddy asked once more.

I was beginning to dislike Buddy excessively.

"It's too much time and trouble to do anything else. With any luck, nobody'll find them in time to identify anybody."

"But what if they do?" Buddy persisted.

"I've got a plan B," Cal said curtly. "But I'm not gonna discuss it in front of them. Just in case they manage not to starve to death fast enough."

He turned his back on us and began to trot toward the house. Mrs. Banducci yelped a protest at the rough handling as Buddy grabbed her again and steered her toward the back of the truck where the double doors stood folded back.

He didn't bother to put down the lift to get the old lady into the truck. He picked her up and dumped her inside, eliciting another bark of objection from her, and then Bo did the same with me. At the same time, I saw the hidden car move out from behind the house.

I recognized it immediately. The old black beater we'd seen cruising the streets at Lofty Cedars before we'd even moved in. So they'd been casing the neighborhood, looking for places where people were buying new stuff like TVs and computers and furniture they could get good prices for when they sold it.

And then Bo slammed the doors on us, and we heard the bars falling into place, locking us in.

For a moment we lay there, breathing hard, in the darkness. It was pitch-black, no crack of light showing anywhere.

Moments after they shut the doors on us, the old vehicle began to move forward. We didn't go very far. When we stopped, I listened intently for voices or the sound of the old black car, but I couldn't hear anything.

"Have they left us here? Are we alone?" I asked in a hushed voice. Though if we couldn't hear them, they couldn't hear us, either.

And then Mrs. Banducci said, "Well, come on, Kaci Drummond. Roll over here and see if you can untie me."

For a seventy-eight-year-old lady, Mrs. Banducci was pretty gutsy.

"Rolling's not easy when you're wearing a backpack and your hands have been tied together so long they feel like they're going to fall off," I said, deciding it would be more practical to maneuver onto my knees and then kind of scoot on my face toward her.

"What's in that thing, anyway?" Mrs. Banducci wanted to know. She didn't sound as petrified as I felt. "You carrying any lunch, by chance? I only had coffee for breakfast because I was expecting my friend, and it's long past lunchtime. My stomach's rumbling."

Lunch. Food was the last thing I was concerned with, but I had packed a lunch for school, the way I always do. "I have a ham sandwich with mustard, an apple, and two oatmeal cookies," I told her. "And a granola bar I was planning to eat on the way home."

She made a sound of approval. "Let's get these ropes off and get at it," she said.

It took an interminable time to get Mrs. Banducci untied. The ropes were tight, I couldn't see the knots, and my fingers were painfully numb. Once in a while she'd say something like, "I made an apricot coffee cake this morning. My friend loves it." Or, "That Bo fellow has bad breath, did you notice?"

Mostly I just sweated and grunted as I fumbled behind me while we sat back-to-back. At one point I broke a fingernail, and it stung where it tore down into the quick. I didn't have the luxury of time to rest and wait for the pain to ease. I gritted my teeth and kept working at the knots.

When they finally came free, I grunted in exultation, though of course we were still locked inside a truck that had been abandoned and hidden under some trees in the hope that nobody would notice it or investigate.

"I haven't been bound up that way," Mrs. Banducci declared, "since my brother Tommy tied me to a tree when I was eight. We were playing Joan of Arc, and he went off to find kindling to put around my feet so he could burn me up. Mama wouldn't let him take any matches out of the house, and he got hungry and stopped to fix a snack and forgot all about me. It wasn't until suppertime when I didn't come in to eat that he remembered where he'd left me. He got his butt blistered for that one, I'll tell you. Served him right." She moaned a little as she rubbed her chafed wrists, apologized for taking the time to do it, and began to work on my knots. "Speaking of suppertime, it might be easier for me to undo these ropes if we took the backpack off. Can I unfasten a strap or something and do that before I get you untied?"

I agreed it would be a good idea, but hoped she wasn't going to want to find my lunch and eat before she accomplished the important thing, and she didn't. Since she was working with her hands in front of her, even though she still had to contend with pitch-blackness, she did the job much more quickly than I had.

I brought my hands around front and rubbed circulation back into them. My torn fingernail hurt, and I sucked on that finger for a minute, then bit off the loose part of the nail as best I could. Finally I reached for the backpack, but Mrs. Banducci had already felt her way into it.

"Ah, here's the sandwich," she said with satisfaction. "You don't mind if I help myself to half of it, do you?"

"Help yourself to all of it," I invited. "I've always thought it was crazy to make a big deal out of a last meal before a prisoner is executed. What good is it? Whose stomach would be settled enough so you could swallow and not have it all come back up?"

Surprisingly, Mrs. Banducci chuckled. "We're not dead yet, child. Put that good young brain of yours to work and think of something. What else you got in this backpack thingy?"

"Books, papers, and the rest of my lunch," I told her. In the short time she'd been our next-door neighbor, I'd thought she was kind of a pain with her nosiness. And of course if she hadn't been overly inquisitive this morning, she'd never have been captured after letting the air out of one of their tires and peeking in the windows of our house. But I was glad I wasn't locked in the back of this truck by myself.

"You sure that's all? It felt heavier than that when I lifted it, unless you've got an awful lot of books. Why don't you feel around it and see if you can't find something else that might be useful. I'll bet you've never completely emptied it out since you got it, have you? Hmmm. I thought you said this was a ham sandwich."

"It is. With mustard. I made it myself."

"It smells exactly like peanut butter." She paused to take a bite. "Ah! Ambrosia for a growling stomach! Peanut butter and jelly."

"It can't be," I said, scowling to myself in the darkness. "I made it . . . oh, no!"

"Nothing wrong with peanut butter and jelly," Mrs. Banducci assured me. "Are you wrong about the apple and the cookies, too?"

I knew what had happened. Mom had told Grandma she shouldn't have picked identical backpacks for Jodie and me, because we'd mix them up. Grandma had responded, rather tartly, that they hadn't had any pink ones for Jodie, so she'd had to get two red ones unless we wanted dirt-colored ones like the boys'.

Mom still makes Wally's lunches, but the rest

of us do our own. We usually make them the night before and get them out of the refrigerator in the morning. And this morning—a million years ago!—Jodie had left the house before I did and picked up the wrong backpack. In fact, I thought she'd sneaked out early because she was up to something again and didn't want to get caught or questioned. I hoped she hadn't been hiding the fact that she was wearing my newest blouse. And then I remembered that it didn't matter much, considering the circumstances. If she'd left anything in the backpack that would get us out of this, I'd forgive her for swiping anything.

"It must be my sister's bag," I said. "I can't imagine what there would be in it that would be of any use in getting out of this truck. Not even Jodie is likely to carry a can opener or a cannon to blow a hole in the side."

I could smell the peanut butter, and it was making me nauseous.

"Well, it won't be much comfort when they find our bodies," Mrs. Banducci said cheerfully, "to find that there was something in that bag that would have kept us alive long enough for someone to rescue us. You sure you don't want half this sandwich?"

"No, thanks," I said. But I took hold of

the backpack she pushed toward me and reached inside to check it out.

There was an apple. And a packet that was undoubtedly cookies. And a plastic bag with something squishy in it. A small tube of something I couldn't identify. Had she borrowed some of Mom's makeup? And then my fingers touched something that sent my spirits soaring.

At my cry of triumph, Mrs. Banducci stopped chewing. "What?" she demanded. "What did you find?"

# nine

"A phone! Dad's cell phone! I thought the thieves had taken it, along with our other phones, but Jodie had put it in her backpack! The little sneak!"

I remembered how Jodie had wanted to go somewhere after school and asked to take the phone. "Mom wouldn't let her use it. None of us is supposed to take it off Dad's desk, but she knew neither Mom nor Dad would be using it today, so she just swiped it. She probably figured she'd put it back before they came home and they'd never miss it. She'll be in real trouble when they find out." I paused, remembering how glad I was that we'd found it. "Or maybe not, since it may save our lives this time. I hope!"

"A telephone?" Mrs. Banducci was smiling. I could tell, even in the dark, that she was smiling. It was in her voice. "Well, get us out of here, girl!"

I was holding the instrument in my hand and I could imagine it quite clearly. White plastic, with a blue button at the top to press to turn it on. I located the button and pushed. Immediately I heard the reassuring hum of a dial tone.

I nearly cried in relief. Dialing a one would be easy enough. It was the first button on the left, just below the power button. The nine should be the last number on the right, at the bottom. From the top, down the right side of the pad of buttons, three, six, nine. I counted them out. I knew where the numbers were supposed to be, but it made me anxious not being able to see them. I dialed and haoped for the best.

God does answer prayer. At the other end of the line, the phone rang, and a male voice said, "Emergency services."

"The police!" I gasped. "Please, don't hang up just because I'm a kid! I'm in terrible trouble! My name is Kaci Drummond, and I've been kidnapped! Me and my neighbor, Mrs. Banducci! We both live in Lofty Cedars Estates, and . . ."

"Kaci? Hold on, please." There was a totally different timbre in his voice. "I'm going to turn you over to Detective Myrek, all right?"

There were a few seconds of silence, during which I thought my heart would stop if we'd been disconnected. And then a different male voice, deeper, stronger.

"Kaci? This is Detective Ross Myrek. Are you all right?"

"We haven't been injured, but we are locked up in the back of a truck—"

"A yellow bob tail? License number VCT 7258?"

Tears of gratitude filled my eyes. "Yes! You found my message on the wall!"

"Your mother found it when she went to the house to check on you. And we found the note on Mrs. Banducci's desk when her friend called. Can you tell me where you are?"

"I'm not sure. They put tape over my eyes when we were partway here. But when we left our house and got on the freeway, we turned south. I couldn't tell how far we drove, or for how long. It seemed forever. Then we left the freeway, went east over an overpass, and then on for a few miles, and then onto a gravel road. We're on an abandoned farm, with a pretty big barn, where the thieves hid all our furniture and stuff."

"Can you make a guess as to how far south you went on the freeway?"

"All I'm sure of is that when we turned onto

Compton Street, maybe half a mile from the house, the odometer registered two hundred thousand forty-two miles, and we drove a total of thirty-seven miles altogether after that. Does that help? Can you find us?"

His voice warmed. "With that kind of detective work on your part, we ought to be able to pick you up in a matter of minutes. State Patrol Cars are rolling in that area now. And the Channel Four helicopter is in the air, monitoring traffic. We'll contact them, and they'll search for you from the air."

"The truck's almost hidden under the trees next to the house," I said quickly. "But the other sides of the house are in the open. Old, run-down, peeling white paint," I told him. "Two stories high, with a porch all across the front of it."

"Do you know where the kidnappers are?"

"They were going to run the truck into the river, with us in it," I told him. "But we let the air out of a tire, and they didn't think they could get it that far. So they left in an old black sedan. Maybe ten years old; a Chevy, I think. It looked like it had been used hard. We didn't get the license number on that when we saw it; it was too dirty, and that was before they kidnapped us, anyway, so I wasn't looking."

"That's good, Kaci. Now I'm going to turn you back over to the dispatcher. I want you to stay on the line. Tell the operator when you hear the chopper, okay?"

"Okay," I said, sounding shaky.

"I'm standing by," the 911 operator said then. "Let me know when you hear anything, okay?"

"Okay," I agreed. The receiver was slippery in my hand, I was sweating so much.

"Just hang on, Kaci," the operator said, and then I didn't hear anything more.

Except for Mrs. Banducci's chewing—she was now working on the apple—I couldn't hear anything at all.

I drew a deep breath. "We might not hear a helicopter," I said uneasily. "I think this truck is insulated or something. We couldn't hear their voices or the sound of the car when they left."

"I think you'll hear the chopper, especially when it drops low over you," the operator told me. "Don't worry, our officers will find you."

I thanked him, and then reached out to touch Mrs. Banducci in the darkness. "They are sending patrol cars and a helicopter. We just have to wait now."

Her hand patted my knee. "I told you it would all work out, didn't I?"

"I think you said at your age you didn't spend

much time worrying about dying. I couldn't be as calm as you were. I've been praying almost steady."

"So have I," she said. "Only sensible thing to do, under the circumstances. But I'm a firm believer that God helps those who help themselves, so we had to try everything we could, like letting the air out of their tires. Is it all right with you if I eat one of these cookies?"

"Go ahead," I said.

"You want the other one?"

"No, thanks. When we get out of here"—I very carefully didn't say "if" we got out—"I'll probably be starving, but right now the thought of food makes me queasy."

"So. What were you doing home in the middle of a school day?" she wanted to know.

"I was having an allergy attack and I went home to get my nasal spray." I'd forgotten my running nose, and I was breathing all right now. "My mom must have come home on her lunch hour and found the license number of the truck where I'd written it on the wall. And your friend called 9-1-1 when she saw your note."

"I knew she would. Sarah's a sensible woman. She's been my friend since we were your age. So many years ago! I met her when I fell through the ice when we were skating, and she helped rescue me. She fell in, too, before her brother got there with a two-by-four from a nearby construction site, and we both wound up with hypothermia. I got pneumonia, too. You don't forget friends like that."

"No, I don't suppose you do. Do you hear anything yet?"

"Nope," Mrs. Banducci said. "If you're sure you don't want this last cookie, I think I'll eat it."

And, then, suddenly, we did hear it. Faintly at first, and then coming closer.

I spoke into the receiver excitedly. "I think I hear the helicopter!"

"Good," the operator said. "Stay on the line." I could hear him relaying my information to someone else.

The sound grew quickly louder, until we could tell it was right over our heads. And then something entirely unexpected happened.

The double doors at the rear of the truck were thrown open, leaving us blinking in the sudden sunlight.

Mrs. Banducci's excited exclamation of "They found us!" died in midbreath.

Because it wasn't the police. It was Cal and Buddy and Bo.

I know what the word "consternation" means. I had never felt it before, at least not like this.

They were mad. And they were scared. A dangerous combination, Dad would have said.

The helicopter was directly overhead, its noise thunderous, and its blades were stirring up dust and the leaves on a nearby tree even though the thing was still high overhead.

It only took a few seconds for my eyes to adjust to the sunlight after the blackness inside the truck. I couldn't hear sirens over the racket of the chopper, but I saw the first of the State Patrol cars turn off the main road a short distance away, and then another one, churning up dust on the long driveway, red and blue lights flashing.

Cal and his friends were aware of those cars, too, undoubtedly about to be here in seconds. Why had our captors come back? I wondered frantically, and then realized that the police were chasing them. They must have been spotted as soon as I talked to the detective, and they'd decided their best chance was to return to us and depend on making the authorities back off if we were held up as hostages. I was horribly afraid that it might work.

In the meantime Bo was looking into the truck at us, and he had a long-bladed knife in one hand.

The stuff I'd dumped out of Jodie's backpack was scattered all around me. Nothing for a weapon to stall them off, nothing at all. An empty sandwich bag, an apple core, and the phone, which I was still clutching.

I dropped the phone. I couldn't hear the 911 operator's voice anymore, but I knew he must be able to hear the chopper, although it was pulling away now, lifting higher into the sky. I scrabbled beside me in the junk to reach anything I could that I could throw at them.

I wish I could say I reasoned it all out, but I didn't. Dad said later I was just going on instinct in trying to protect myself. I was so scared, it was a miracle I could function at all. The police were so close—but Bo had a knife, and they'd wanted me as a hostage before to shield themselves in a situation like this. I only knew I had to try anything to hold them off until the cops could reach us, before Bo put that knife to my throat, or to Mrs. Banducci's. If they threatened to kill us if the cops didn't let them leave, would the police be able to stop them?

I had no doubts now that when Bo and Cal and Buddy were through with us, when we were no longer of any use to them, they wouldn't hesitate to kill us.

The plastic bag that had felt squishy inside the backpack was beside my left hand, filled with gold sequins Jodie had been going to glue onto something at school. I felt it pop open when I squeezed it, and glittering bits sprayed out into the air. Pretty, but worthless.

My right hand closed around the little tube. Glue—that's what my fingers were touching—glue to stick glitter onto something, a costume, maybe.

I picked up the glue—sort of like arming myself with a feather to fight off a cougar—and instinctively slid backward, away from the three menacing figures already bounding up into the truck.

The chopper had retreated enough by now so I could finally hear the approaching siren of yet a third patrol car. The first two had driven right up to us, and uniformed officers were leaping out of them, weapons in hand, yelling at the menacing trio to stop where they were.

Actually I wasn't consciously taking all this in at the time. My heart was pounding so hard, my chest hurt, and panic was making me deaf and blind all at once. But I remembered, later, the welcome sight of uniformed police officers with drawn guns, even as I feared they wouldn't be able to stop whatever Calvin and Bo and Buddy intended to do.

I didn't realize that they couldn't kill us in the next few seconds, because then we wouldn't be hostages any longer, and the police would have no reason to hold their fire. Fear had turned my brain to Silly Putty—or so I thought at the time.

As Bo jumped up into the compartment where they'd kept us prisoner, I felt the little tube in my hand. I don't remember twisting the cap off, but there must have been a small part of my mind that wasn't paralyzed by fear.

And as he lunged toward me, where I was sprawled in the middle of the junk from Jodie's backpack, I squinted and held out my pathetic little tube and squeezed it as hard as I could. Right into that snarling face.

It was only a tiny tube. There wasn't much in it. At first I thought it hadn't had any effect at all, and then Bo swore and swiped at his face and went down on his knees and roared in anger. That gave me time to slide a bit farther away. Beyond him, Buddy was wrestling with Mrs. Banducci, who, for an old lady, was putting up a pretty good fight. Cal had already gone down under a swarm of blue uniforms.

I felt the knife fall against my leg and slide off onto the floor of the truck. Bo started to scream and he had both hands on his face. "What did you do to me, you—" Whatever he was going to call me was cut off when an officer hauled him backward out of the truck where the sound of the helicopter rotors drowned out his cursing.

Another officer helped me to my feet and I was lifted down onto the ground, where my legs were almost too shaky to hold me up.

Two other officers had gone to the assistance of Mrs. Banducci. Overhead, the Channel 4 chopper was tilting for a better angle of what they'd show on the six o'clock news, and it wasn't until it rose even higher and began to swing away that any of us could hear what anyone else said.

Bo was still screaming and writhing around. "My eye! She squirted something in my eye, and my hand's stuck to my face!"

The officer who was holding on to my arm bent his head so I could make out his words. "What was it, Kaci?"

I handed over the squashed tube and read the label the same time he said it out loud. "Super Glue! Oh, boy, that's going to require a trip to the hospital. That's wicked stuff. He may not be able to get his eye open if it really got it. Better call an aide car for that one, Jim. That Super Glue sets in thirty seconds. They can use it to close an incision these days."

They led him away from me, still mouthing obscenities, and they rounded up the other two and put them into the back of one of the patrol cars. Then they installed Mrs. Banducci and me in another one.

"You want this?" one of the officers asked, handing in Jodie's backpack with all her junk packed back into it.

Everything but the phone. He kept that long enough to make contact with the 911 operator, who was apparently still on the line, to give him a report. Then he handed it over to me. "You did some pretty quick thinking there, young lady."

"It didn't seem like I was thinking at all," I admitted. "We thought they were gone. I never dreamed they'd come back!"

"They panicked when they found they had a patrol car on their tail. We were looking for a car of that description, and I was about to pull them over and check them out when they swerved onto an off-ramp, turned around, and headed back here. They undoubtedly figured that having you and Mrs. Banducci as hostages was their only chance of getting away. You did a good job of holding that one off so he couldn't put that knife to your throat. You just sit back for the ride home. Your folks are waiting for you at headquarters."

"I suppose it's too late for lunch with Sarah now," Mrs. Banducci said. "She probably went home."

By dinnertime my appetite had come back. Mom picked up Chinese takeout—she was too  nervous and exhausted to cook, she said—and neither she nor Dad went back to their jobs that day.

Jodie knew about the switched backpacks of course. For one thing she'd had to eat my ham sandwich instead of her own peanut butter and jelly, and she was pretty nervous about the stuff she had taken. She wasn't supposed to have the Super Glue, either; as Mom pointed out, it was much too potent to use to stick sequins onto a costume. Actually, none of us was supposed to use it without supervision.

And in spite of the fact that the phone had proved invaluable to me, she got bawled out for taking it and the glue. She almost always got away with whatever she did, and ordinarily it would have been sort of satisfying to see her on the spot for once. Not that I expected it to change her in the long run. But I was surprised to realize that I felt almost sorry for her as she explained while Mom and Dad were both watching her with those incredulous expressions on their faces.

"Why the telephone, Jodie?" Dad demanded.

My sister licked her lips and glanced at me as if for help. I was even more astonished to hear myself saying, "Well, it *was* a good thing it was in the backpack when I needed it."

"Yes," Dad agreed. "We're grateful for that

part of it. But we still want to know what she expected to do with it."

Mom had a sudden flash of understanding. "You were taking it somewhere so that you could call me after school, weren't you? You weren't going home, you were going where there wouldn't be a telephone."

Jodie squirmed on one of the kitchen chairs, the only ones left in the house at the moment. She looked at me again, but I didn't see any way to help her. In fact, I couldn't believe that I even *wanted* to help her. I felt like I ought to say *something*, just to show that for once we were both on the same side, but nothing came to me.

"Bethany and I were going out to the lake where they're making the movie," she said in a small voice. "We thought maybe they'd let us be extras in the mob scenes. The paper said they'd need a couple of hundred kids, and they'd pay them twenty-five dollars apiece." She swallowed hard. "Mrs. Wightman wouldn't take us out there, either, and said Bethany couldn't go. We . . . we didn't think anybody'd ever know the difference, if we were home before suppertime."

Mom's voice was quiet. "And how were you going to get out there if nobody took you?"

Jodie licked her lips again. "On the bus. There was one, right after school got out."

"You knew it was wrong, didn't you?" Dad asked. "Both to take the phone and to deliberately disobey your mother?"

Jodie chewed on her lower lip. "Yes," she admitted.

Dad's a school principal and is good at handling kids who get sent to the office for misbehavior. He didn't bawl her out anymore. He just sighed and said, "Think about this the next time you decide to do something you know we don't want you to do, Jodie."

He and Mom stood up, then, and went to take care of something or other, leaving me and my sister sitting at the kitchen table. I was even sitting on the chair where I'd been tied up and scared to death.

Jodie was close to tears as she looked at me across the table.

I cleared my throat. "I'm going to watch a new video tonight. I mean, it's an old movie, a Hitchcock one. It's supposed to be pretty scary, but you can watch with me if you want to."

She brightened a little, swiping at a stray tear that had escaped onto her cheek. "Okay," she said, even though I knew that getting scared wasn't her usual idea of fun.

Afterward, she said she was nervous and wondered if I'd let her sleep with me that night instead of in her own room. And she actually said that blue and white were restful colors for a bedroom.

We eventually got our furniture and silver and pictures and all the other things back. The broken glass was replaced in the kitchen window. The number I'd written on the wall washed off. There was a tiny scratch on Jeff's baby grand, but Dad got it touched up so it hardly showed. The bedspread they had wrapped around the piano got torn, so Mom and Dad had to get a new one. As long as they were doing that, Mom ordered new draperies for their bedroom, as well.

We heard that the doctors got the glue off Bo's face and hands, though I guess it was an uncomfortable process. We learned later that he was related to another new family in Lofty Cedars, the Burgers. He'd visited them with his folks and then mentioned to his friend Cal that there were a lot of TVs and computers and sound equipment going into those new houses. And Cal had suggested that he and Bo and Buddy might manage to steal some of it while the families were all out working. They had done a number of jobs together before they came to Lofty Cedars Estates and hadn't been caught. No one suspected them until they came to our house.

There was a story in the paper, of course.

Everybody in town read all the details. That didn't stop the kids at school from asking me to repeat them. By the second day, I was totally tired of the entire subject; I just wanted to forget what had happened. I prayed I'd never have that kind of adventure again as long as I lived.

Luckily, it didn't spoil my love for adventures in books. I just got a new one from the library today. It's by an author I haven't read before, Edward Bloor, and it's called *Tangerine*. That doesn't sound like a mystery, but the blurb on the cover sounds intriguing.

But I won't read it when I'm alone in the house. There are limits to everything. I'll have a big bowl of popcorn, all to myself, and I'll choose a time when Mom and Dad are downstairs, right close by.

I might even ask Jodie if she wants to come to my room and listen while I read the new book aloud to her. I might make a mystery fan of her yet, who knows?